Just One Summer

A Summer Romance Novella

A.D. Justice

JUST ONE SUMMER.

BOOKS BY A.D. JUSTICE

Steele Security Series
Wicked Games (Book 1)
Wicked Ties (Book 2)
Wicked Nights (Book 3, by September 2015)
Wicked Intentions (Book 4, Date TBD)
Wicked Shadows (Book 5, Date TBD)

The Crazy Series
Crazy Maybe (Book 1)
Crazy Baby (Book 2)
Crazy Love (Book 3, Date TBD)
Crazy Over You (Book 4, Date TBD)
Drive Me Crazy (Book 5, Date TBD)

Dominic Powers Series
Her Dom (Book 1)
Her Dom's Lesson (Book 2)

Completely Captivated *(Stand-alone, Date TBD)*

Just One Summer *(Stand-alone Novella, August 2015)*

SPECIAL THANKS

First and foremost, I want to thank my Lord and Savior for His continued forgiveness of a sinner.

To my husband: I love you. Thank you for putting up with the late nights, time away from you, and all your support.

To my Street Team: Thank you for being my beta readers, my sounding boards, my biggest supporters, and the best all-around people in the world. Love all of you.

To my readers: Thank you for taking a chance on an indie author. I love hearing from everyone, so stop by my page and say hello.

To my assistant: Tabitha Charisse, thank you for all your help and support.

To my BFFs: I don't know how I managed to do anything right before I met the best friends anyone could ever ask for. A.M. Madden and Michelle Dare, I love both of you.

To the bloggers: None of this would be possible without your help, support, and tireless pimping. I love everyone in this great group of people. I can't name one without naming everyone because you've all been so helpful and wonderful friends.

CHAPTER ONE

JAGGER

JUNE

It's Friday night and the music is thumping as I walk into the club. The bass is cranked up so high that the whole floor vibrates with every beat of the tempo. It enters my body with each step that carries me farther inside. The dance floor is packed with hot, sweaty, barely-clad bodies. People writhe in time to the beat and are acting out the suggestive lyrics. Hands grope strangers in the dark before they wind their way through the masses to a hidden corner in the back of the club.

I smile to myself when I watch another twosome disappear around the corner. I've lost count of how many girls I've taken back there after finishing our set. So many girls use vacation as an excuse to go wild, fuck some stranger, and brag about how romantic he was when they get home to their girlfriends. They do it even more so when they bed the lead singer of a popular local rock band in said vacation mecca.

Here's the raw truth. I pour my heart and soul into my music. I give my all to the crowd while I'm on stage. Making my fans feel like a valuable part of the show is important to me because there's no doubt about who supports my dreams. Once I step off the stage, though, I'm a normal twenty-five year old guy. When a beautiful, drunk girl walks up and strokes my dick before I even know her name, I don't waste time romancing her. We go to the dark hallway in the back of the club and I fuck her brains out. Then I'm done with her and I walk away.

My band is named after me, Jagger York. Yeah, my parents were big fans and carried it a little too far. It could've been worse though. The girls seem to like it and there's no doubt they like me. My good genes were inherited from both of my parents. I'm easily six-foot tall, with a natural athletic build, without looking like a muscle head. The ladies love to run their fingers through my thick black hair and stare deeply into my dark brown eyes.

So as I walk through the club toward the tables where my friends are congregated, there's no shortage of barflies who try to get my attention. Without even time to order a drink yet, I've had no less than half a dozen girls try to get in my pants. No one can tell me that men are the dogs, always sniffing around for something to hump.

I take my seat with the guys in my band and several of our mutual friends that are here with their girlfriends or dates. I approach the table and receive a rousing round of welcomes.

"About fucking time you got here. Where the hell have you been?" Dane, the lead guitarist, scowls.

"Dickhead. Can't believe you've left us waiting all this time," Tanner, the drummer, adds.

Wes, the bass player, just flips me off and returns to making out with the girl beside him.

"What's the big fucking deal? You're all here, having fun without me. Why do I have to be here at a certain time?" I ask.

"We were supposed to meet with Joey about renewing our contract here," Tanner replies, clearly disgusted with me.

"Shit, man. I completely forgot that was tonight," I admit. "I'll talk to him and smooth it over."

"If you get us kicked out of here, I'll kick your ass," he replies.

'Here' is Club Deviant, one of the hottest nightclubs in the South Beach area. It's hopping here year-round, but summer brings vacationers from everywhere. Losing our spot in the lineup is not an option and I definitely fucked up. But Joey is a good guy and he knows we pull the crowds in.

"Don't sweat it, man," I dismiss him.

A waitress walks by and I touch her arm to stop her. She flashes me a seductive smile and obviously thinks I've stopped her for a different reason. "Hey babe, can you bring me a beer?"

Her smile falls as she nods. "Sure, Jagger. Be right back."

When I take my seat, I finish saying hello to our entourage of friends. The most gorgeous girl I've ever seen takes a seat with us and I lose my voice. Her hair is a gorgeous chestnut brown with blond highlights. I can tell from here that her eyes are a deep blue that rivals the depths of the ocean. She's obviously new to the club scene from the uncomfortable glances she keeps throwing at the dance floor.

When I finally move my eyes to see what she's looking at, I stifle a laugh when I see the couple dry humping a few feet away from us. Cutting my eyes back over at her, the expression in her eyes as she watches them changes. For a split second, I think she wishes she were the one having that much fun. She quickly masks her desire and turns her gaze away from them.

She's sitting next to Vince's date, Jennifer, and leans over to whisper something to her. Jennifer smiles, nods her head, and they both stand to walk off together. I'm sure I look like one of those exaggerated cartoon characters, with my eyes bulging out and my tongue unrolling across the floor like a fucking red carpet.

The dress she's wearing hugs and accentuates her hourglass figure in all the right places. Her breasts are perfectly round and just the right size to fit in my hands, just like her ass. Her legs are long, lean, and muscular. *Fuck me.* I think I'm drooling on myself.

I move over to the vacant seat beside Vince as casually as possible. "Hey, man. What's up?"

Vince chuckles before he takes a swig of his beer. "She's out of your league, man."

"What? Who?" I try to play it off.

"You know who. The girl you've been staring holes into for the past five minutes. The girl that just walked off with Jennifer. Her name is Mali Greyson. And she's *way* out of your league," he stresses.

5

"What makes her out of my league?" I'm offended by my friend's assessment of me.

"She's not a whore dog for one," he grins. "She's nice, and she's a good girl. Not your type. Too good for you."

"That hurts," I reply.

"It would if you had feelings," he retorts.

"What's the deal with her? Why do you say she's a good girl?"

Vince's hand freezes midair, his bottom jaw is slack, and his eyes grow wide. "I don't fucking believe it. You don't recognize her. Or even her name."

"Man, I meet all kinds of girls and never even ask their names. Why would I know hers?" I sneer.

"Just thought you may recognize the daughter of one of the best music producers around. Guess not," he shrugs.

"Holy shit! Her dad is Milo Greyson?"

"The one and only," he replies. "Jennifer went to school with her, they lost touch, and found each other again on Fakebook."

"I don't remember ever seeing much about her in the tabloids," I remark.

"And you won't ever. Milo keeps pretty tight reins on her. He knows firsthand how those fuck 'em and leave 'em rock stars are,"

Vince pins me with his words. "He won't let his baby girl date them."

"She's all grown up now," I point out as the waitress returns with my beer.

"Yeah, she's grown. But she's still a trust fund baby, dude," he shakes his head. "You honestly think she'd risk a lifetime of wrath from Daddy just to spend one night with you?"

I take a drink from my longneck bottle and drain nearly half of it in one gulp. He does have a point there, but I'll never admit that to him. There's only one thing that stops me from putting him in his place. Mali Greyson is approaching and I'm completely tongue tied again. My eyes, however, move without a hitch and they are drinking in every detail of her.

Childhood fairytales convince little kids that love at first sight is real. The man and woman look into each other's eyes, feel the instant connection that bonds them for life, and they're instantly soul mates. The man swoops in, saves the damsel in distress, and he instantly hangs the moon in her eyes.

That's all bullshit. Every last word of it. I watched my mom and dad tear each other apart with their malicious words and conniving backstabbing all through my childhood. I compared those fairytales to real life at a young age. By the time I hit puberty, I swore off 'love' and replaced it with 'lust.'

A girl falls in lust at first sight and then convinces herself that it's true love. She believes they're meant to last forever and can weather any storm. That line of thinking is what fucks up more people than anything. Believing in a lie and trying to live up to the high standard established in our formative years.

Knowing that, I saved myself from all the heartache that my friends suffered. Any girl who hooked up with me knew the drill. Our trysts would only last for a short time and when I stopped calling, she knew not to chase after me. A couple of girls thought they could change me, make me fall in love with them, and turn me into their fairytale ending. Those girls know better now.

With that in mind, I realize that I've fallen into a very deep and serious case of lust for Miss Mali. It's more than her beautiful face and her smoking body. I sense a completely different vibe from this girl. She's confident but reserved. She showed up here without a date, as a third wheel with Jennifer and Vince, but she's not at all awkward about it.

Her beauty outshines the hundreds of other girls in this club, but she seems approachable. She can't be a complete prude because she likes watching the dirty dancing from the sidelines, but she doesn't indulge in it for very long.

I'd bet my last dime that I could bring out the wild cat in this little tame kitten.

"Mali, this is Jagger York. He's the lead singer of the band," Jennifer introduces us. "Jagger, this is Mali, a good friend of mine from school. I just found her after all this time, and she's only here for a little while before I lose her again," she says, as she throws her arm around Mali's neck.

"Hi, Jagger," she smiles, revealing her straight, perfectly white teeth. "It's nice to meet you."

I reach for her hand, raise it to my lips, and place a soft kiss on it. "Nice to meet you, too, Mali," I reply. "How long are you in town?"

"Just for the summer," she replies.

"That's definitely long enough for us to get to know each other very well," I suggest with a wink.

Her warm, friendly smile changes into a knowing smile. One that confirms that guys hit on her all the time, attempt to be charming, but she sees straight through their bullshit. It also tells me I'd better change my tactics before she completely kicks me to the curb.

"Can I get you a drink?" I offer nicely. "My beer is about gone, so I'd be glad to get yours while I'm at the bar."

"Sure," she smiles.

Her smiles change with what she's thinking and give her moods away, but I don't think she realizes it. Knowing what I know about her father, I'd guess that he's expected her to act a certain way in public. Always polite. Always cordial. Never give the public a reason to think badly of her. But, inside, she wants to say what she really thinks.

This smile she's giving me now says she's plotting. No doubt that she's about to try to embarrass me or put me in my place with her drink order. That's okay, wildcat. Keep showing me what you think you're hiding so well. Two can play this game.

"I'd like a shot of 'Cock Sucking Cowboy' and a 'Suck, Bang, and Blow' chaser, please."

Oh, she's good.

But I'm better.

"Coming right up." I emphasize each word and hold her gaze a second longer than normal.

There's no way in hell I'm ordering a 'Cock Sucking Cowboy' for anyone. But I'll get her something she'll love even more than that. After I weave through all the drunken revelers, I get the bartender's attention and order our drinks.

I keep from smiling too broadly as I walk back across the crowded club with our drinks in hand. One shot, one mixed drink, and a beer. The anticipation of seeing her face when I tell her what I have for her is killing me.

"Sorry, but they're all out of butterscotch schnapps. This is the second best 'Screaming Orgasm' you'll ever have. Good news is, you can have all the 'Screaming Orgasms' and 'Suck, Bang, and Blows' you can take," I say, as I lean in close to her to deliver her second drink.

Her chest heaves with her excitement, her hooded eyes drop to my mouth, and her fingers brush mine as she takes the shot glass from my hand. She's definitely affected by the blatant innuendo, she likes my dirty talk, and she wishes I'd continue. But she doesn't want to be the one to ask.

No, wildcat, you won't ask me at all. But you'll soon beg me.

"Th-thank you," she stammers.

11

"Any time," I reply casually. I don't want her to know that she affects me, too.

Now is the time to build up the tension in her, make her come to me. As I walk back to the end where my band mates sit, I take my time and make idle chit chat. Her eyes are fixed and locked on my every move. Before I make it back to my seat, a couple of girls grab my hand and try to pull me on the dance floor with them. I politely decline but make it a point to kiss the back of their hands like I did Mali's.

When I finally sit, my eyes flit over to look at Mali and I meet her gaze. She doesn't look pleased. Her eyes cut away from me and find the two girls dancing together in the crowd. She first narrows her eyes at them, then she rolls her eyes in disgust and shakes her head. She throws her head back and swallows her 'Screaming Orgasm.'

Did I just detect a hint of jealousy? Nice.

Dane, Tanner, Wes, and I throw back a few beers and just shoot the shit for a while. Our conversations keep me engaged so much that I don't even think about giving Mali a second glance. When I finally glance up, Joey Andrews, the club owner, is walking toward us.

"Nice of you to join us, York," he smirks.

"There's nowhere else I'd rather be," I laugh.

"I need you guys to do me a favor. Our DJ has to go home early and the other one can't get here for another hour or so. Can you take the stage and fill in the dead air?" Joey asks.

"Sure," we all agree. "About that contract extension," I add.

"Consider it done," Joey dismisses me. "Like I'd let you leave anyway."

Joey is an older man, somewhere between my dad and my grandfather's age. He considers all of us as his sons, looks out for us when we need it, and kicks our asses when we deserve it. We couldn't ask for a better employer.

"Thanks, Joey. We really appreciate it," Dane replies.

"You're up in ten," Joey says before he walks off.

"Well, I smoothed it over with Joey," I announce to the guys with a smirk.

Vague threats to remove my balls and use them as hood ornaments on cars go in one ear and out the other.

We take the stage for an hour and play our hearts out. This is what we do best and the crowd here loves us. When the lights swing over the crowd, I'm more than pleased to see

Jennifer, Vince, and Mali dancing and having a good time on the dance floor. Mali has the moves, I'll give her that. When the backup DJ takes over, I may have to get her out on the dance floor myself.

"So, what'd you think?" I ask Mali as I take the seat next to her when our set is over.

"It was great," she replies enthusiastically. "I really love your sound. You've created a very unique mixture of rock, pop, and soul."

"You have a good ear," I compliment her. "Most people wouldn't have picked that out."

"Comes with the family name, I guess." She's clearly sizing me up, and checking my intentions for talking to her.

"Names have nothing to do with it. That talent is all yours," I answer. The beginning chords of a slow song start and I feel the need to abruptly change the subject. "Would you like to dance?"

"I'd love to," she replies.

As I stand, I take her hand to help her up and then lead her to the dance floor. She willingly steps into my space as she wraps her arms around my neck. My hands slide around her waist and we begin swaying to the music in tandem. The way her body fits against mine is pure heaven. I plan on getting to know Mali Greyson much better over the next few weeks.

As the song ends, Jennifer weaves through the crowd in our direction. "Mali, Vince and I are leaving now. Are you riding back with us?"

Jennifer's gaze skims up to mine. Her silent warning screams at me. My reply is to simply smirk at her.

"Yes, I am," Mali replies. She turns to me before she walks away. "Thanks for the dance, Jagger."

This is already shaping up to be quite a summer.

CHAPTER TWO

JAGGER

It's been one week and a day since I last saw Mali. I've tried to get Vince to give me her number a couple of times, but he claims he doesn't have it. He also refuses to ask Jennifer for it. I can't say I blame him, since she carries his balls in her pink purse and only lets him use them once a year.

We're back at Club Deviant for our regular set tonight and the place is packed to the gills. The line to get in is wrapped around the building and it's already at maximum capacity inside. I love nights like this because everyone is here to have a good time. The adult libations are flowing and two inebriated bodies magically become synced as one when the couples reach the dance floor

"Let's get onstage, boys," Tanner says as he stands.

The guys begin checking their instruments, tuning them, and checking the sound levels. I grab the microphone and start my own round of tests.

"Who's ready for some sex, alcohol, and rock and roll?" I yell into the microphone.

The crowd screams their reply of a resounding yes. Their deafening roar is enough to raise the roof. People rush toward the stage, but a line of girls somehow always makes their way to the very front. They dance provocatively, sing along with the lyrics, and slowly lick their lips when I look in their direction.

Ah, the rough life of the lead singer.

"We have a new lineup of songs for you tonight. Is everyone ready to get dirty?"

The cheers and screams come from every corner of the club. I love this part of my job. Sharing my music is as close as I get to sharing my heart with anyone. It's part of me and I freely give it away to the masses.

"Let's get everyone on the dance floor and have some fun. The more people to bump and grind with, the better. Right?" I laugh and the crowd screams again.

Tanner ticks off the count with his drumsticks and both he and Wes kick in the bass line. Dane adds his lead guitar licks to the mixture and the crowd begins swaying in time with the music. I begin belting out the lyrics and visualize the scene as I sing it to pour emotion into it. I move back and forth across

17

the stage to engage the audience and energize the room.

Arms reach out to touch me and I slide my hand across theirs as I walk by. Some try to grab me and hold on, but I've learned to be quick in my movements. When I stop to sing to someone, to emphasize the words and drive them wild, I know to stand well out of reach.

When we reach the end of our set, the dance floor is packed with hands, arms, legs, and bodies stacked from front to back. There's barely room to move, much less walk, but no one seems to mind at all. Strangers rub against each other as they sway with their partner. There's a new level of erotic being created in the air tonight.

I don't know how, but movement in my peripheral vision catches my eye. Cutting my eyes to the left, I now know what triggered it. Mali is trying to cut through the crowd, her eyes set on me. She has that same expression she had last week– the one she had when she tried to hide her desire.

Some random guy snakes his arm around her waist and pulls her close to him. He grinds his crotch into her ass, his fingers dig into her hip to hold her, and she struggles to break free from him. Her look of desire quickly turns to panic as this guy changes the movement of his hips from a circular motion, to front to back, like he's fucking her from behind.

Something in my mind snaps when her pleading eyes find mine. She's begging me, but in a different way than I've imagined repeatedly. She's scared, she can't get away from him, and although they're fully clothed, he's still molesting her body against her will.

Instantly, I drop the microphone and it releases a screeching sound that makes people grab their ears in pain. When I leap off the stage, the crowd parts like the Red Sea to give me plenty of room to stalk toward my target. My expression must be near murderous because the girls gasp as I rush by them and the guys crane their necks to get a good view of the action.

The idiot with his hands on Mali is apparently too distracted by his friends cheering him on to notice me. When he finally looks up, his bottom jaw drops open in shock and fear just before my fist connects with his ugly face. His head jerks back violently as his feet forget to work, causing him to stumble a couple of steps backward before he falls on his ass.

A split second before he falls, I grab Mali and pull her to me so he can't take her down with him. She wraps her arms tightly around me, her body trembles from fright, and her knees buckle underneath her.

"I got you. Hold on to me." I murmur against her ear, as I scoop her up in my arms and carry her off the dance floor. She wraps her arms around my neck, lays her head on my shoulder, and hides her face against my body.

Wes and Dane are close behind me when Wes calls for club security. They saw what the guy did to Mali and relay the whole story to the head bouncer while I keep walking with Mali in my arms. The bouncers surround the guy and his friends as they all deny the accusations.

Jennifer and Vince watch me with a mixture of amazement and horror as I approach them with Mali still cradled in my arms. They're frozen to the spots where they stand as they try to comprehend what just happened. I'm still running on adrenalin, or I'd be overanalyzing the situation, too.

"I'm going to put you down. You're safe now," I tell Mali, intentionally keeping my voice soft to avoid scaring her.

She replies by squeezing my neck tighter. She holds on to me with all her might. The only reason I want to put her down is because I only got to hit that fucker once before he went down. He needs his face stomped for what he did.

But Mali won't release me.

MALI

I'm holding onto a man I met a week ago, and only spoke a few words to, like he's the only lifeline I have in this world. It'd be different if I actually knew him, but other than a short conversation and a slow dance, I don't know him at all. Part of me is embarrassed to be in this predicament to begin with, while the other part of me is just scared to death and wants someone to make me feel secure again.

"Mali," his voice soothes. "You're okay now."

Reluctantly, I loosen my grip around his neck and allow him to stand me up on my shaky legs. I look up at him and give him a rueful smile. "Thank you, Jagger," I tell him with all sincerity. "You didn't have to punch him out, but thank you for helping me."

"No need to thank me for that. I have a little sister. If any man touched her like that without her permission, his body would never be found," he says emphatically.

I nod, understanding exactly what he means. "I'm going to the ladies' room to clean up a bit. I'll be right back." I need to get away from the small group of friends crowded around me.

Jennifer gives me her concerned mother look. "Do you want me to go with you?"

"No, thanks anyway. I'm okay," I reply and try to give her a confident smile.

I'm shocked to find the bathroom completely empty when I enter. No women's bathroom is ever empty, but especially not one at a club like this. *They must all be waiting for Jagger*, I think to myself. I rush into the stall, lock the door, and have a complete breakdown. The feeling of being helpless and violated floods me. My imagination runs away with me when I think about what could've happened if Jagger hadn't stopped him.

When I hear the door open, I hold my sniffles and sobs so no one knows I'm falling to pieces in here. The voices hesitate in the doorway as the girls drunkenly yell at someone else. They're giggling uncontrollably when they finally enter and the sounds of them having fun help to lighten my own mood. My face is still such a mess from crying, so I decide to wait in the stall until they leave.

"Oh my God! Did you see Jagger deck that guy?" one yells from the stall on my right.

"Yes! How fucking hot was that?" comes the reply from the stall on my left. "Have you ever seen Jagger fight over a girl before?"

"Hell no!" right drunk girl replies. "The only F word I've ever seen Jagger do for a girl is fuck her!"

They both cackle at what they think is the funniest joke they've ever heard. I've heard better.

"Why did he have to fight for that bitch anyway?" left drunk girl asks. "Why didn't she just turn around and smack that guy herself?"

"I know, right?" right drunk girl replies. "It's not like he had her somewhere alone. He didn't even have his hand under her clothes. What a little crybaby bitch. She needs to grow a pair so she can take care of herself and quit depending on a man to do it for her."

Dual flushing halts the conversation until they both stumble out of their stalls. I can still hear them talking about me over the water running in the sinks.

"And how did a girl like that snag Jagger anyway? What's so special about her?"

"Maybe he secretly likes the sweet, innocent, helpless type. That's the only difference I see in her. Every other girl I know has tried to snag that man, but they're not little scared pussies," she says before laughing at her own words. "I just called girls, pussies!"

The door opens and their voices trail off into the distance and more girls come rushing in together. I open the stall door and walk to the sink before they have a chance to start a conversation about me. When I look up in the mirror, their cruel words swirl around in my mind.

Do others really see me as a helpless victim?

Am I so sweet and innocent that sexy, worldly men like Jagger don't see me as dating material?

Is that why he equated me to his sister a few minutes ago?

Staring into my eyes in the reflection, the hard truth slaps me in the face. I don't want to be that girl. The one who is scared to do anything that's exciting, daring, and dangerous. The one who needs to be saved and can't look out for herself. The one who has to settle for a man who's willing to take care of her because she isn't strong enough to stand on her own two feet.

After cleaning the dried tear streaks from my face, I pinch my cheeks to bring some color back to them, put on my best face, and confidently stroll back to my group. As I approach, several faces turn toward me and I instantly see the pity and worry openly aimed at me.

I don't want to be the girl who is pitied.

I want to be the girl who is envied for her strength and boldness.

Looking from face to face, the one I want to see the most is conspicuously missing. "Where's Jagger?" I ask Jennifer.

"He said he wasn't finished with that guy who put his hands on you," she inclined her head toward the crowd. "He went back for more."

I jerk my head to the right and see a significant crowd has formed a circle around something. My first guess would be that Jagger is in the middle of that circle and he's about to pummel the other guy. Normally, I'd stay as far away from a scene like this as I could get.

But my new leaf was turned over when the words those girls said in the bathroom cut straight through me.

CHAPTER THREE

MALI

Marching over to the crowd, I elbow my way inside and step into the human ring. Two of the bouncers are holding Jagger back from the guy who touched me. His lip is busted and bleeding, his eye is swollen, and his cheek has a huge, red mark quickly forming. Jagger's face doesn't have a single mark on it.

"Let me go, Jim," Jagger growls at the bouncer.

"No way, Jag. That's enough, man."

"What's your fucking problem?" the other guy yells at Jagger. "I was just dancing with a girl and you attacked me for no reason."

"Shut your fucking mouth, Chad," Jim yelled at the douchebag guy. "You keep taunting him and I'll accidentally lose my grip on him."

Chad looks worried for a second as he considers how angry Jagger still is. He turns to walk away and his eyes lock onto mine. His slow perusal of my body makes me feel cheap and dirty, but I realize that's his intent and I refuse to allow him.

"You want to feel this again, baby?" he derides me as he grabs his crotch.

I'm not a victim.

I'm not helpless.

I return his gesture as I allow my eyes to slowly rise and fall as I take in his unremarkable features. My expression conveys my disgust with him. Out of spite, my eyes lock on his crotch and I release a laugh that both mocks and humiliates him.

Meeting his gaze directly, I deliver my zinger. "I've already felt all you have to offer, *baby*. Believe me, I'm not impressed. You're not man enough for me."

The crowd erupts in laughter and I laugh along with them. Chad's face turns red from embarrassment and anger. He takes a step toward me and Jim instantly releases his hold on Jagger. Chad must sense it, or maybe he sees Jagger moving from the corner of his eye, because his head whips around as his feet halt.

Chad then turns and rushes through the crowd and Jagger stops short and yells to him. "You better run, you little pussy! Show your face in here again. I dare you."

Jagger turns and calmly walks to me. "Are you okay?"

27

"I'm fine. You really didn't have to go after him again," I tell him.

I actually feel bad that he's fighting my fight when I don't even know him. And when he only sees me as his scared little sister. I want to say I can take care of myself, but we both know that's not true.

"He deserved it. I wanted to give him everything he deserved," Jagger shrugs, like it's no big deal.

"His face looked like he definitely got that," I chuckle.

"You seem to be in better spirits," Jagger smiles, and the all-male beauty of it nearly knocks me down.

I noticed him the instant he first walked in the club last week. His confident swagger caught my eye, but everything else about him captivated my attention. It was nearly impossible to not stare at him as he talked with his band members. His thick, black hair is spiky, stands up haphazardly in every direction, and looks incredibly sexy on him.

He's built like a natural athlete. He's not blown up like he's on performance enhancing drugs, but his biceps are well defined. His shoulders are broad, and his muscle shirt hugs his chest and abs like a second skin. His jeans

28

hang low on his hips and fit perfectly to show off his long legs and ample ass.

I've thought about him every day for the past week. I've wondered what he does when he's not on stage. My list of questions about him grew with each passing day. Given the chance, I'd go back in time to last weekend and tell Jennifer to leave without me. But I was too scared to chance a one-night stand a week ago. And I was too chickenshit to ask Vince or Jennifer for Jagger's phone number.

But tonight when he started singing, he obviously put me in a trance because my feet unconsciously carried me to the dance floor. My eyes were set solely on him and I wanted to be one of those girls that he sang to in the front row. When Chad first grabbed me, I naively didn't think much about it. There were so many people on the dance floor, it was impossible to not touch or be touched as I wound my way through.

I panicked when I realized what he was doing, though. The fear and uncertainty shut me down and locked me up. I'd been watching couples dirty dancing from afar, wishing I were that bold and carefree. Wishing Jagger would sweep me up and teach me how to enjoy it. But the real thing felt much different than my fantasy. Plus, it wasn't Jagger doing it with me.

Now he's standing here with me after defending my honor. All I can think of is marring it by recreating the scene with him instead.

"I had a long talk with myself," I admit, to my amazement.

His eyebrows slowly rise as he considers my confession. "You've been talking to yourself?" A small smile plays on his full lips, but he refrains from making fun of me.

"Yes," I smile. "I actually had a good, long talk with myself."

"And what did you and yourself come up with?"

"We've decided some major changes are in order. Me and myself, that is."

His smile crawls across his face, reaches his eyes, and sends my pulse racing. "This I can't wait to hear."

"We have a proposition for you. Are you willing to help us out?"

"Why do I get the feeling that I'll be the dead cat from my intense curiosity?" he asks with his sexy smirk intact.

I shrug but keep eye contact with him. "Why did you just answer my question with a question?"

"Because you're making me nervous," he admits.

Equal mixtures of thrill and panic surge through me from his words. I make him nervous? No, it's definitely the other way around.

"Well, if you're too scared," I sigh and intentionally look away. When I turn to walk away, he grabs my hand and holds me in place. I turn my face to look at him directly again and the fire burning in his eyes warms me inside.

"Let's hear your proposition," he commands, with his voice strong and sure.

I turn completely toward him and take a half step closer. Even though we seem to be lost in our own world in this conversation, we're still in the middle of the club, on the dance floor, and people jostle into us from all sides. "Come by my condo tonight so we can talk about in private."

He hesitates a little too long for my comfort, but I wait him out as if it doesn't bother me at all. "I'm not sure that's a good idea."

"How do you know if I have a good idea or not? You haven't heard it."

"I meant it's not a good idea for me to go to your condo tonight," he clarifies.

"I know what you meant, Jagger," I reply while giving him the *duh* look. "But if you're so positive you don't want to, I certainly won't make you."

When I turn to leave again, I realize he's still holding my hand. I pointedly look at his hand clasped around mine before I look back up at him. He's breathing harder and his nostrils flare with each forceful exhale. He's fighting his desire for me, but I won't help him with that. I quickly jerk my hand from his grasp, smile, and walk away.

From my peripheral vision, I see he's still standing in the same spot where I left him after I tell Jennifer and Vince goodbye. I pick up my handbag and make my way out of the club. I can feel his eyes track my every move, watch my every step, and I know he's waiting for me to look over my shoulder to give him one last, longing look.

I don't oblige him.

When I step out into the humid, night air, I inhale deeply and move toward a waiting taxi. The driver is leaning up against the car and watches me approach him. "Do you need a taxi?" he asks.

"Yes, please," I reply.

He opens the car door for me to get in and I hear my name being called from behind me.

"Mali, hold up a minute."

I throw him a bored look over my shoulder. "What do you want, Jagger?"

"Your address," he sighs. "I'll probably end up regretting this, but I know I won't get a wink of sleep until I find out what this idea of yours is."

It's my turn to make him wait for my answer. I pretend to take a few seconds to think about it and give him the impression I'm having my own second thoughts.

"Fine," I sigh. "But don't waste my time. If you're not there within the hour, don't bother coming at all."

I rattle off my address to him and watch as he realizes it's in one of the most prestigious buildings in the area. The cab driver clears his throat to get my attention so I slide into the back seat. Jagger's dark brown eyes follow me as the cab pulls away from the curb.

My silent prayer is that my plan actually works.

JAGGER

I pace back and forth on the sidewalk outside the club while I think about her request. *Come to my condo so we can talk in private.* If I go to her condo, talking will be minimal and only about the things that I want to do to her. Or what I want her to do to me. Or what we'll do to each other.

If I don't go, my overactive imagination will forever torture me with vivid scenes of what her proposition is. My gut says she'll request something insane. And for one fucking reason or another, I'll actually agree to it and later kick myself repeatedly for my stupidity.

But if I don't go to her, I'll go home with someone else from the club and work out all my sexual frustrations on her instead. Then I'll leave before she even wakes up and my sanity will remain intact. That's the option I should go with. It's the safest route and the one with fewest variables.

It's not the one I'll fucking choose though and I damn well know it. I know I'm walking straight into a trap but I'm going to do it anyway. Shaking my head, I stomp off to my truck and drive to her condo on automatic pilot.

When I pull up to the gated entrance, I wonder if she's already given my name to the guard. He opens the door to the security hut with his clipboard in his hand, and gives me a suspicious look. "Name?"

"Jagger York," I reply. A miniscule part of me hopes she forgot or changed her mind, so the guard will send me packing.

"Miss Greyson is expecting you," he confirms and presses the button to open the gate. "Have a nice night." His tone leaves no doubt that he knows I'm here for a late night booty call.

I don't know if I should be more worried that he's right, or that he's wrong.

After finding a parking spot, I walk to the elevators and ride to the penthouse suite of this ultra-swanky complex. When I ring the doorbell, it takes a couple of seconds before I hear movement inside. The sounds of the deadbolt and doorknob being unlocked do nothing to settle my sudden case of nervousness.

When Mali opens the door, my nerves dissipate and all I can think about is where I'll put my mouth first. She's wearing a short, silky white nightgown. The material both flows over and hugs her shapely body. Her erect nipples press against the flimsy material and cause an uncomfortable tightness in my jeans.

"Come on in, Jagger," she says casually, as she turns to walk toward the couch. The material barely covers her perfectly firm ass cheeks and stops just low enough to tease me with the hope of a sneak peek. "Have a seat."

She sits and pulls her legs up on the couch. She leans them over to the side as she puts her weight on one hip. The fabric of her nightgown stretches across her chest, further accentuating her breasts. My eyes travel down her torso and take in her beauty. I can't recall a time before when I've felt so stupid and so enraptured with a woman.

Intentionally sitting across from her in the chair, I keep my expression passive. "So, why am I here, Mali?"

"Tonight has been very eye opening for me," she starts. "First, that guy Chad humiliated me on the dance floor in front of everyone, but no one around me would help. Until you jumped off the stage.

"But even before tonight, I realized that I haven't really been living life. My parents sheltered me so much and kept me away from anything they considered unpleasant. It's good in a way, but in another way it robbed me of being able to function in those situations.

"Anyway, when I went to the bathroom to collect myself, a couple of girls came in and said some things about me that were really hard to hear. Their words hurt at first, but when I realized how right they were, that hurt even worse."

She stops talking for a minute to gauge my reaction. So far, I haven't heard anything I think I need to respond to. She had an epiphany about herself tonight. Good for her. Does she want a medal?

"I asked you to come here tonight because I think you can help me change a few things about myself. You have quite a reputation for being a ladies' man, of being fearless, and taking risks others wouldn't dream of taking.

"I'm here for the summer and all I'm asking for is your time. Spend just one summer with me to help me do the things that scare me. To help me step out and live life just for the sake of living. To be my 'for a good time, call' teacher."

I'm literally stunned speechless for a minute. "Let me get this straight. You said a lot, so I'm going to paraphrase and you let me know if I'm on target."

"Okay," she agrees.

"You want me to teach you how to be the female version of me?"

CHAPTER FOUR

JAGGER

Am I on hidden camera? This has to be the most well played practical joke and I'm the ass-end of it. There's no way she's really asking for a summer full of one-night stands with me. Vince was right when he said Mali is a good girl. She just thinks she wants to be bad, to be different from what she's always been. That's why her reply stuns the shit out of me.

"Yes, exactly that," she confirms. "Except I don't want to sleep with a bunch of different guys. That's not what I mean. I only want it to be with you. Can I have one summer, just one summer, with you, to learn to let go?"

"So, you're not fucking any other guys all summer. And you expect me to not fuck anyone but you all summer?" I ask.

"Is that so bad?"

I detect the hurt tone in her voice. "It's not that you make it bad, Mali. I just don't do monogamy very well. Or at all, actually."

"I'm not asking you to fall in love with me. That's not what I want either. I'm leaving at the end of the summer. I have my own plans and career goals. But I want to really live my life while I'm young. I know myself too well, Jagger. I won't take that leap without help," she pleads.

I rake my hand through my hair and quickly stand. Disappointment covers her face when she thinks I'm about to walk out on her.

"You're putting me in a really tough spot here, Mali. I mean, *look at you*. Of course I want to do this with you. But spending the whole summer with one person, when I've never wanted to be tied down to one person for even one day, is a lot to consider." My frustration has me pacing back and forth again.

Then a thought hits me. A way out. She'll tell me to fuck off and I can leave knowing it wasn't my choice.

"What do I get out of this?" I ask.

"What?" she asks incredulously. "What do you mean by that? You'll get me."

"No, *you'll* get *me*," I emphasize. "My time, my advice, and my instruction. What do I get in return?"

She looks perplexed for a moment and I draw up to my full height. My triumph over this insane proposition will fall from her lips

39

any second now when she concedes she has nothing to offer me. I cross my arms over my chest and wait for those magical words.

"I'll make sure my father listens to your music," she says. "I can't guarantee that he'll produce you, but I can promise that he'll hear your songs and make his own decision."

She could easily knock me over with a fucking feather. If a breeze were to blow through this condo, I'd be knocked the fuck out. She used her ace in the hole to trump my faceless card. I stare at her and wait for her to laugh, say she's kidding, and that I can leave now. But she doesn't.

"Is that good enough?" she asks meekly.

Why do I feel like a lamb is being led to the slaughter, and I'm the lamb?

"That's good enough," I nonchalantly reply. She just used the very thing–the *only* thing–that could make me agree to this ludicrous idea. "But this is for just one summer. This is not forever after. This is not a happily ever after fairytale. This is not a couple of people who suddenly realize they're madly in love and can't live without each other."

"I completely agree," she nods. "This is you teaching me how to overcome my inhibitions and experience all the things I'm too afraid to try on my own."

"Tell me something. Why me?" I ask, genuinely interested in her answer.

She looks down at the floor, too embarrassed to admit her reason.

"Mali. First rule is, you have to be completely honest with me, no matter how embarrassed you are to say it. That's the only way I can give you what you need," I explain.

"Jennifer told me a lot about you on the way to the club last week," she replies with a shrug, but she doesn't finish that thought. "She was actually warning me about you. But there's just something about you. And tonight when you stopped that guy, I felt safe with you. But being around you also makes me feel dangerous. Reckless. Impetuous," she confesses.

"Ah, now I see. The bad girl you've repressed underneath that good girl image wants to come out and play. And I'm the one who can unleash her," I summarize.

"Yes," she whispers, desperation lacing her tone.

My knees nearly give out when she answers. Her one word holds more desire, more need, and more longing than the forward advances from all the other girls combined.

For the first time since I hit puberty, I don't know what to say or where to start.

I feel like a fucking fish out of water, so I decide to do what I do best. My fingers grip her hand and pull her to stand directly in front of me. My knuckles graze her cheek and continue down her long, slender neck until I reach the dip at her collarbone.

Lengthening my fingers, I use the tips to lightly brush against the skin along the base of her throat. On a downward stroke, my index finger flows over her silky smooth skin. I continue moving over the silky smooth fabric of her nightgown, moving slowly between her breasts, and down her taut stomach.

Her breath hitches in her chest as she inhales sharply. Her lips part as she lightly pants with anticipation of what I'll do to her next. My hand stills just as I cross the top of her lacy panties and I intentionally hold it there. I want the heat from my hand to physically make her burn with desire.

"What do you want me to do next, Mali?" I ask, in my take-charge-alpha-tone. The tone that says I know what she wants, but I expect her to verbally admit it.

"What do you want to do?" she replies and tries to turn it back on me.

Slowly, I shake my head from side to side but keep my eyes locked on hers. "No, ma'am," I tsk her. "Consider this your first test. If you don't pass the test, I'll be on my way home. Now tell me, Mali. What do you want me to do next?"

"I want you to kiss me," she responds. "Show me you can't get enough of me. Like you're dying for a single drop of water in the hottest desert and only I can quench your thirst."

Her request really isn't that far-fetched. I've wanted to get lost in her mouth, and in her body, since I first laid eyes on her. Moving my hands to cup her cheeks, I slide them to the back of her head and thread her hair through my fingers. When I crush my mouth to hers, all that is innately Mali floods my senses.

Her sweet flavor invades my mouth while her sensual perfume conquers my sense of smell. She steps into me and her soft, voluptuous curves press against the hard muscles of my body. I feel her soft moans resound through my chest as our tongues meet. For the first time in a very long time, I'm genuinely concerned that the zipper of my jeans won't be able to withstand the growing pressure behind it.

Breaking the kiss for a minute to breathe, we're both reluctant to put too much distance between us. My lips hover just above hers as my body begs for just one more taste, one more touch, and one more minute of sheer delight. What's really off the charts right now is, I'm more focused on getting one more mind-blowing kiss than I am on fucking her.

What the hell is wrong with me?

My fingers skim up her arms, grip her shoulders, and turn her away from the couch. Using my body to control her, I walk her backward until she meets the wall. My arms slide around her waist as my mouth covers hers again. She willingly meets my vigor as her tongue strokes mine. She pulls me to her and the weight of my body pins her to the wall. My hips surge up involuntarily and demonstrate my utter lack of control. She whimpers and grips my shirt in her fists when the bulge in my pants grinds into her clit. Her fingernails dig into my skin as the kiss and the dry humping become more forceful, needy, and consuming.

"Stay with me tonight," she simultaneously asks and states when she pulls her lips from mine.

"I'd love to," I reply. "But I can't stay tonight."

She jerks her head back and looks at me like I've just slapped her. "Let me guess. You have company coming early in the morning and you really need to get home and get your beauty sleep," she says sarcastically.

"That's almost all true," I tell her. "My parents and my sister are coming to stay with me. I'm not the best housekeeper, so I really do need to be there to pick up before my family gets here. The only thing you're wrong about is the beauty sleep part. I think I'm good on that for a while."

"Are you serious? Your family is really coming and it's not that you just don't want me?" she asks softly.

Sliding her hand down across my crotch, I smirk. "How can you possibly think I don't want you?"

She surprises me when she doesn't move her hand away. "That is a persuasive argument," she replies breathily.

"Come by my place tomorrow morning around ten and hang out with me. You can meet my family. If we're going to be together all summer, we need to get the introductions over with sooner rather than later," I offer and give her my address. "They visit me quite a bit during peak season."

"Okay," she nods. "I'll be there. Good night, Jagger."

"Goodnight, Wildcat." I chuckle, give her one more smoldering kiss, and hightail my ass out of her apartment before I change my mind.

I'm in a daze as I leave Mali's condo. This is insane but I can't stop myself. What is it about this girl that has me reacting to her so differently than I have any other? I've never jumped off stage and pummeled a guy like that before. And after it was all over, I even went back to give his mouth another taste of my knuckle sandwich. When I saw his hands on her, I lost my shit like never before.

There's a perfectly good explanation for this. She's a witch, an enchantress, a sorceress, and she's put a spell on me. There's no other plausible reason why I just walked into a blatant trap with Milo Greyson's daughter. Yeah, he can definitely make my career. But he can just as easily break it. Even now, knowing that, my head keeps telling me to turn this truck around and go back to her apartment. It's a good thing the head on my shoulders is the one making the decisions tonight.

As I climb into bed alone, I'm kicking myself for not bringing Mali home with me tonight instead of telling her to come in the morning. I could've spent all night memorizing every inch of her body, the sounds she makes, and what she likes the most. "That's it. I'm fucking calling her and telling her to come over now," I tell the darkness.

Then I realize that I didn't get her number before I ran out of her condo and I groan loudly. "Just great. Now I have to call Jennifer myself since Vince won't ask her. She'll put my balls in her pink purse, too, and I'll only have yearly visitation rights."

CHAPTER FIVE

MALI

After Jagger left my condo last night, I tried to go to sleep but ended up tossing and turning more than anything. As I thought back over our conversation, I realized how pathetic and desperate I sounded and decided to call the whole arrangement off.

It's now seven a.m. and I'm running on a total of maybe two hours of sleep and an entire pot of coffee. I'm so far beyond mortified at my behavior that I don't think I can face him today. My only excuse is the alcohol clouded my judgment and I suffered from temporary insanity. The view from my balcony helps clear my head and I have no doubt that fate helped me dodge a huge bullet last night.

When I usually have to cancel plans with someone, I call, apologize profusely, and explain the situation. Since I didn't get his number before he left last night, I can't call or even text to say I won't be there. I only have his address, which is completely stupid of me and further proof that I wasn't thinking clearly.

It's too early to call Jennifer and ask for it. But even if I do, I can't explain why I need it. She'll think I hooked up with him, he snuck out while I slept, and I'm chasing him now. Or, she'll think that I want to hook up with him and I'll never hear the end of it after she warned me off of him on the way to the club that night.

While I try to determine how to handle this, I decide to take my shower and get dressed. I'm wide-awake and won't be able to sleep anytime soon anyway. The hot water spray feels so good as it massages my neck and shoulders. That's when it hits me, the solution to this whole mess.

There's no reason for me to call or text him. No reason for me to have his phone number at all. He'll probably be relieved when I don't show up. My stupid idea isn't something he willingly wanted to do anyway. Besides, he probably wouldn't have lived up to his end of the bargain. I shake my head at my own naiveté.

"Yeah, as if a guy like Jagger York would settle for being with only me all summer."

By the time I finish dressing and styling my long brunette hair, it's almost eight a.m.

and I haven't had a bite to eat. My stomach was in knots at just the thought of facing Jagger today, but it just growled at me and demanded food. When I bounce into the kitchen and pour a bowl of cereal, my cell phone alerts me to a new text.

As soon as I open the text from a number I don't recognize, my appetite completely disappears.

Hey Wildcat, this is Jagger. Don't even think about standing me up. My place. 10 a.m.

Shit.

I quickly type my reply.

Hey there. How did you get my number?

Jagger: Woke up Vince and Jennifer

Me: You're brave. Jen's not a morning person.

Jagger: Found that out the hard way–lol

Now is my chance to tell him I'm calling this whole crazy idea off. All I have to do is make my thumbs type the words. I start typing and quickly delete. I start again but those words aren't right either. As I start typing a third time, I see the three little dots that tell me Jagger is sending a message.

Jagger: I thought about your idea all night...

I hold my breath as he continues typing.

50

Jagger: Hardly slept at all…

Same here, Jagger, I think but don't respond. He's typing again.

Jagger: Very original. You shocked me…

He's doing this on purpose. Teasing, tempting, and pulling me into him. His plan is definitely working.

Jagger: You probably sensed my hesitation…

Here it comes. He's going to dump me before this goes any further. Disappointment floods me, despite the fact that I've unsuccessfully tried three times to say it to him first.

Jagger: But it's a brilliant idea. So quit trying to get out of our deal and get your ass over here.

Wait. What?

Jagger: You're not backing out on me. I'm all yours for the summer.

Oh shit. Oh shit. Oh shit.

Me: How did you know?

Jagger: Come over and I'll tell you.

Me: Now?

Jagger: ASAP. Bring your bathing suit.

Before I change my mind, I save his contact information in my phone. I grab my bathing suit, slip on my flip flops, and hop in my Infinity G37 convertible. I key his address in my GPS and put the top down for the drive to Jagger's place in Coral Gables.

It doesn't take long before I pull into the driveway of a gorgeous, single story Spanish Mediterranean home. There are immaculately landscaped flower and shrub beds, the grass is perfectly lush and green, and walkways connect the front and back yards. It's like an island sanctuary and I'm thoroughly enjoying the scenery when the front door opens.

Now I'm enjoying the scenery for a very different reason. Jagger stands in the doorway—shirtless. My eyes devour his bare chest and his well-defined abs. I let my eyes follow the happy trail from his navel to his denim shorts, down his muscular legs, and to his bare feet.

He clears his throat conspicuously and my eyes fly up to meet his. "Wildcat, if you keep looking at me like that, we won't have any time to talk first."

My face heats with my intense embarrassment and I drop my chin to my chest. I hear his chuckle before he softly calls to me. "Get over here, Mali."

My feet hear his command and they take over where my brain fails me. His hand under my chin lifts my face until I'm looking into his

52

chocolate brown eyes. "I'm glad you're here," he says sincerely. "Come inside."

He steps to the side to give me room to pass and I walk inside. I hear the door click behind me and I turn to look at him. He leans against the door, blocks my exit, and continues to speak.

"I had my doubts that you'd actually show up. Thought I'd have to toss you over my shoulder and bring you myself."

"How'd you know?" I ask. My curiosity always gets the best of me.

"Things usually look different in the light of day, especially after you've had time to sleep on it. You second-guessed yourself because what you really want is contrary to what you've been taught. Change is uncomfortable, and we all gravitate to what's comfortable.

"I knew if I stayed last night, you'd wake up today and regret it because you'd made a rash decision in the heat of the moment," he explains. "But, you made a conscious decision to come to me today. So make your final decision now and stick to it. Just know that whatever you choose, there's no changing it later. What do *you* really want?"

He just put the ball back in my court. His text said he wouldn't let me back out on him, but he's giving me the power to decide. I have the feeling when he said I can't change my mind later, he actually means his offer is a now or never kind of deal. He won't be here if I say no and later change my mind.

What do I really want?

"I don't want to back out on you," I admit. "I want to go through with our arrangement. Should we discuss the rules?"

"Sure. You go first," he smiles. He knows this conversation makes me uncomfortable.

"I know I said it last night, but I can't stress this enough. If you can't handle complete monogamy, I won't even start this," I insist.

He tilts his head to the side, narrows his eyes, and flashes the sexiest half-smile I've ever seen. "Deal," he says with a slight nod. "I have a feeling you'll keep me so busy I won't even have time to look."

"Your turn," I urge.

"This is the one rule I can't stress enough. Do not get attached to me. We're not falling in love, getting married, having kids, and living happily ever after. You won't change my mind on this, so don't even try," he bluntly asserts.

"Deal," I agree. "Can we not tell your family that we're basically just fuck buddies, though? That's embarrassing for me."

54

He inhales deeply as he considers my request. I know I've just asked him to lie to his family, but I can't help but think that's the lesser of two evils. "Fine. I'll tell them you're my girlfriend, but my sister will see straight through it. Don't be surprised when she calls bullshit to your face."

"Thanks for the warning." I purse my lips to the side and give him a dubious look.

"I'll push you past your boundaries. Regardless of how uncomfortable you feel, you can't run away from me," he stipulates.

"Fine. Anything else?" I ask.

He pushes off the door and crosses the floor to stand directly in front of me. He's taller than I am by at least six inches so I tilt my head back to look him in the eye. "Two more things, actually," he whispers as his arms circle my waist. "One, you have to trust me. I'd never physically hurt you."

"And two?" I ask on bated breath.

"Two," he lowers his lips to mine. "I can kiss these lips whenever I want."

"You know, Jagger, you don't have to 'wine and dine' me," I reply. "I'll keep my end of the deal and get my dad to listen to your music."

"I know you will, Mali. I just really want to kiss you again," he murmurs against my lips.

He urgently pulls me to him and takes full possession of my mouth. His lips are so soft but also so insistent. His tongue seductively licks the part in my lips before he completely takes control of my body. His hand slides over my breast, his thumb stops when it finds the beaded tip of my nipple, and his calloused pad caresses it through the fabric of my shirt. My fingers curl into his flesh when he increases his pressure.

He slides his hand downward, across my stomach, into my shorts, and strokes the sensitive skin beneath the band of my panties. "Touch me, Mali," he urges me between kisses.

I slide my hands over his chest and across his stomach before I reach the button of his shorts. I easily unbutton and unzip them with a gentle tug, slip my hand inside, and firmly wrap my fingers as far around him as they'll go.

He moans into my mouth when I slide my hand from base to tip. His hand moves further down, to the apex of my thighs, and his finger lightly brushes over my clit. The urge to take control of his hand becomes overwhelming. I begin to push his shorts down with my other hand when the sound of chimes ring throughout the house.

His motions still and he groans in frustration. "My mom and dad are here. They're too fucking early," he growls.

Those words are the equivalent of pouring a bucket of ice water over both of us. I back away from him and straighten my clothes simultaneously. "What?" I hiss. "Oh my God! Button your shorts back!"

Jagger laughs as he adjusts them. "Okay, okay. Keep your panties on," he winks. "My shorts don't exactly hide everything, you know."

I'm the one who needs to find somewhere to hide. Maybe I'll go out the back door and come back around to the front door in a few minutes, and pretend I just got here. Except my car is outside. Shit!

"Calm down," Jagger says as he casts a sideways glance at me. "It's not a big deal."

Jagger walks to the front door and swings it wide open. A shorter, younger, female version of him squeals in delight. "Jagger, I've missed you!"

He gestures to his crotch, then jerks his thumb over his shoulder toward me before he shrugs nonchalantly. "I've missed you, too, sis. I'll have to take a rain check on the hug, though."

She snickers and peeks around him to get a good look at me. Jagger looks over his shoulder and winks at me while flashing the most devilish smile I've ever seen. His parents are both full of smiles, and maybe even slightly hiding their mirth at catching us in this state. I am beyond mortified as I cover my face with my hands for a second. Jagger, of course, looks so pleased with his shenanigans.

I'm going to kill him as soon as his family isn't looking.

"How's my boy been?" his mom asks as she pats his cheek.

"I'm good, Mom. Come on in," he steps to the side and puts me in full view.

"Hey," his sister approaches me with obvious curiosity. "I'm Cass, Jagger's sister."

"Hi, Cass. I'm Mali Greyson. It's nice to meet you," I reply. I don't have it in me to add the *'I'm his girlfriend'* lie to my introduction. Although, it'd probably be better than the introduction he just gave me.

Cass turns to question Jagger with her eyes. His mom and dad both wait for him to elaborate. He smiles widely at me as the words roll off his tongue. "Mali is my girlfriend, Cass."

She gasps and her head swings between the two of us several times before she's able to speak again. "I'll believe it when I see it."

And it's started.

"Don't be ugly," their dad chastises her. "Hello, Mali. I'm Dwayne, Jagger's dad. This is Marlene, Jagger's mother."

"Hello, Mali," Marlene adds.

"Hello Dwayne, Marlene. It's very nice to meet all of you," I reply with a smile.

"Make yourselves at home," Jagger says. "You know where your bedrooms are."

Cass eyes us suspiciously as Jagger moves behind me and wraps his arms around my waist. His chin rests on my shoulder and his cheek is pressed against mine. He slightly turns his face toward mine and places a soft kiss on my cheek. Playing my part, I curl into him and cover his arms with mine.

Cass nods absently before she follows Dwayne and Marlene down the hall toward where I assume the bedrooms are located. Jagger whispers in my ear and cold chills instantly cover my arm. "If you don't spend the night with me, she'll know we're lying. You'd better plan on staying."

What have I gotten myself into?

CHAPTER SIX

JAGGER

"What's going on with those two?" I ask Cass in a brusque whisper, jerk my head toward my parents, and furrow my brow.

She rolls her eyes before she answers. "It's sickening, right? They haven't been able to keep their hands off of each other for the past six months." She mockingly gags as she points her finger in her mouth. "I keep chanting 'one more semester in college' in my head. It's totally unfair that you never come home and share in my pain."

I chuckle and shake my head. "We've had this discussion before, little sister. I had them alone for the first three of years of my life. They're all yours now."

"What's wrong with them?" Mali asks with an incredulous laugh. "They love each other. You can't fault them for that."

Cass and I exchange glances before I turn to explain the situation. "They never got along while we were growing up. I remember one fight after another during my whole childhood.

Now, they seem like completely different people."

Cass concurs. "It was like a switch flipped one day, and they became all lovey-dovey, and sweet, and gross. Those people in there are not our parents."

I glance around the corner of the kitchen and see my mom sitting in my dad's lap, her arms around his neck, and their mouths locked in a passionate kiss. No child, regardless of age, should be subjected to this kind of abuse. "It's like my whole life has been a lie," I sigh.

Mali openly laughs at my soul-splintering pain. "You're kidding, right?"

When Cass and I just stare at her, dumbfounded, she continues. "My parents separated for a while when I was younger because they fought constantly. If Dad said the sky was blue, Mom would argue that it was actually cerulean. Just being around them was exhausting for everyone else.

"Mom moved out for a while and they seriously considered divorce. My parents even went to a divorce counselor to learn how to avoid scarring me for life. The counselor helped them see they didn't really want a divorce–they wanted a better relationship. No matter how much work it was, Mom and Dad never backed down from the challenge.

"Their marriage is stronger today than ever and they're very loving to each other like your parents are. Maybe Dwayne and Marlene went through something similar." Mali shares her family's story as she watches my parents. Wistful longing brews in her eyes and makes me question what she's really thinking.

"You know, you may be onto something, Mali." Cass reflects on Mali's story and how our parents have changed. "There was a time that they stopped fighting, but they were barely speaking at all. I just thought they were giving each other the silent treatment, which was fine with me. Better that than the constant bickering. That was right before they turned into–*this*," she gestures toward them.

Mali's eyes swing around and meet mine before moving on to look at Cass. "They really look happy together, Cass."

This takes Cass aback and her eyes drift back to the oddly happy couple occupying my couch. "They do look happy, don't they?"

Pulling Cass's attention back to the task at hand, we finish making drinks and snacks for everyone and walk into the den. Mom and Dad stop their impromptu make-out session as Mali, Cass, and I set the plates and glasses on the coffee table.

"This looks delicious. How long were you in the kitchen?" Mom asks disbelievingly as she takes a skewer of fresh fruit chunks from the plate.

"Long enough for you and Dad to steam up my picture window during the heat of summer," I deadpan and Cass snorts.

"If you're having performance issues, we'll be glad to talk to you about it, son," Dad chimes in.

Cass and Mali both snort and quickly cover their mouths. I glare at them before turning my wrath on my father.

"Not funny, Dad." Okay, so maybe *wrath* is a strong word to use with my dad. "Talking about performance issues, which I don't have, with my parents would definitely give me performance issues. Which I don't have."

Fuck. This is going to be a long week with my family here.

"Do you think he's protesting too much, honey?" Dad asks Mom, like I'm not standing right fucking here.

"Well, I didn't want to say anything in front of his girlfriend," Mom shrugs.

"Since she is his girlfriend, I'm sure she already knows," Dad says as he picks up some fruit. "Mali, how long have the two of you been dating? What kind of problems have you experienced with him?"

Mali's mouth drops open and she gapes at my dad. To save her, I jump in to answer for her. "We just recently became exclusive," I vaguely explain.

Dad shakes his head quickly from side to side, dismissing me. "What does that have to do with the price of tea in China?"

"Dad. What?" I ask with frustration as I struggle to keep up with this conversation. "You know what, never mind. Forget I asked that. I don't care what you mean. I don't have performance issues. *We* don't have performance issues. We perform just fine. Can we talk about something else now?"

"Your father and I have been seeing an emotional connection coach. We've learned a lot and we can help you, Jagger," Mom confides. "It's been excellent for our sex life. We got caught having sex in the car on the side of the road the other night because we just couldn't wait until we got home."

I think I may develop performance issues from this visual in my head now.

"Oh my God, Mom. Stop. This is child abuse," Cass groans and covers her ears with her hands. "I'm sure my ears are bleeding now from hearing this."

"So, let's change the subject before Mali leaves and never comes back," I say with an eye roll. "You're staying all week, right?"

"About that," Dad starts and gives me a very bad feeling. "That was our original plan, but we've agreed on something even better. We're moving here!"

Mom and Dad both smile widely. Mom bounces up and down on the cushion as they wait for my excitement to catch up with theirs. They're moving here? What the hell?

I glance at Cass to verify that this is some cruel joke the family is playing on me, but her face confirms she was afraid to tell me herself. Traitorous sibling. "You're leaving Tennessee? And the mountains?" I finally ask with pretend enthusiasm.

"We've decided to live at the beach and vacation in the mountains for a change," Dad explains. "We've done the exactly opposite all our lives, just because that's what we've been comfortable with doing. Coming here to visit you the last several years made us wish for it, and now we're finally doing something about it."

"We only live once, and we should live where we're happiest. Close to our kids," Mom beams.

The smile that's plastered on my face has become a permanent fixture. I'm destined to look like a raving lunatic for the rest of my life because I can't bring myself to break my mom's heart. My head keeps nodding and my mouth is frozen in a scary smile, like an evil clown bent on devouring small children.

"I think that's wonderful news," Mali exclaims. "Being an only child, I've always wished for a big family."

My eyes are throwing daggers at her while my sadistic clown smile remains intact. My fucking head still bobs up and down, agreeing with every word that's said. Is it not clear that my parents are moving to be close to me? Essentially, wherever I move, they will follow. Just to be close to me.

Now that damn song is stuck in my head.

"So, Cass," I turn to her and she flinches at my creepy frozen smile. "You're moving here, too? With Mom and Dad?"

Cass purses her lips as she tries to keep from laughing out loud. "Eventually, yes. I have one more semester of college until I graduate. Only because the class I needed is only offered one semester a year and it was full last time. So, I'll stay in the house until it sells."

"So, to answer your question, son. It looks like we'll be here longer than a week. But we'll try to find our own place as soon as possible," Dad explains. "We don't want to cramp your style, especially with a new girlfriend."

"It's time to go swimming," Mom announces suddenly.

Talk about saved by the bell. Dad gave me a strange look when he said 'girlfriend,' and I really don't want to get into a bunch of questions about her. They know I haven't been serious about anyone in years, since my high school crush that turned into a crushed heart. But that girl isn't the reason why I refuse to settle down.

First of all, I'm the lead singer of a rock band and I have pussy thrown at me left and right. They also throw their thongs and bras at me while I'm onstage singing. But I digress. The point is, there are just too many beautiful ladies to pick just one *forever*.

Secondly, and this is really the main reason, I've seen what love does to people. I witnessed how it tore my mom and dad to shreds when they fought. The daggers they threw with their words stung me to the core. The whole premise of till death do us part would make me willingly go to my grave early. Even seeing them now doesn't convince me that it won't revert back at the first sign of trouble.

"Yeah, let's swim," Cass enthusiastically agrees. "It's a beautiful, hot day out there. No wasting it."

After I show Mali to my bedroom so she can change into her bathing suit, I walk back into the kitchen and wait for her to come out. To avoid suspicion in case my parents come out first, I start preparing the steak, chicken, and vegetables for the poolside grill. We repeat this same ritual with their yearly visit.

"You want to tell me what the hell is going on?" Cass demands.

"Holy shit, Cass," I exclaim at her. "That's a good way to get hurt–sneaking up on a man with a knife in his hand."

"Whatever," she says and rolls her eyes. "I know you, Jagger Alexander York. You do not have a girlfriend. I just talked to you recently about this. We laughed about the clingy biotch who signed up for guitar lessons just to try to get to you at work."

Fuck. I forgot about that conversation. Cass knows it, too. She has always been able to read me like a fucking book.

"So spill it, lover boy. What's really going on here?" She raises her eyebrows and waits for my explanation.

"All right, look," I sigh heavily. "She's a good girl. Highly inexperienced. She wants me to teach her how to, you know, loosen up and have some fun. I agreed to be exclusive with her while she's here for the summer. When the season ends, we end."

Cass looks at me like I've grown a new pair of testicles on my forehead. The look is a mixture of horror and amazement, and it really freaks me out when she has this expression.

"You just confirmed the belief I've held my entire life." She put her hands on her hips. Here it comes. "I'm adopted. There's no other explanation. We cannot be siblings."

"What are you babbling about?" I throw my arms out to the side in frustration.

"Do you honestly think that a girl with no experience can spend the whole summer with you and not become attached? If she has no experience, and wants to 'loosen up'," she makes those mocking air quotation gestures, "tell me how she'll do that from being exclusive with you?"

Cass nails me to the wall with her logic. I didn't even consider this could happen. Mali and I have a deal, an arrangement, an understanding that doesn't include any of this nonsense. Shaking my head, I refuse to believe my sister. "You're crazy," I point at her. "Mali and I have an agreement. She doesn't want the happily-ever-after-lie any more than I do."

"Keep telling yourself that, Romeo," she replies sarcastically. "It won't change anything, but it'll make it funnier to watch your nervous breakdown at the end of the summer when you realize you really do have a girlfriend," she laughs and walks out the back door to the pool.

"Why aren't you in your swimming trunks yet, son?" Dad asks as he breezes by me. His beach towel is draped around his neck, his zinc oxide covers his nose, and he's ready for the pool as soon as he grabs a beer.

"Just getting the food ready for the grill. I'm going to change now," I stall as I wait for Mali to unlock my bedroom door.

"Where is Mali?" Dad asks, reading my mind. He stands in front of the sliding glass door that leads out to the pool and scans the area. "I only see Cass outside."

"Yeah, Mali's still in the bedroom changing clothes or something." I pretend to be too busy to know.

"I like her so far. I'm glad you've finally found someone to settle down with," Dad says thoughtfully. "Your mom and I were beginning to think you'd be a career bachelor and we'd never have any grandkids from you."

"Whoa, whoa, whoa, Dad," I shout. "Way too soon for that kind of talk. If you want grandkids anytime in the next ten to fifty years, you need to talk to your daughter."

"You're the oldest, Jagger. I expect you to lead the way, be the example," Dad slowly turns his head and pins me with is pointed gaze. "Cass looks up to you, as a little sister should. She watches what you do, whether you realize it or not."

He slides the door open and walks out on the deck. After he drops his towel on the lounge chair, his beer on the table, and slides his feet out of his flip-flops, he runs and does a cannonball into the water. His resulting splash completely soaks Cass, who screams expletives at him. They splash each other, laugh, and take turns trying to knock each other off the floats.

Memories from our childhood flash in my mind. Brief glimpses of how our family used to be when we were kids and we all had fun together march along, bringing more feelings with them than full scenes. It was fun. It was good. It was different back then.

It was a long time ago.

Female voices carry down the hallway from my mom and Mali's conversation. As they get closer to the kitchen, I turn to walk toward them so I can change and join the outdoor party. My jaw drops, my feet halt, and my eyes bulge out of my head when I see Mali in her sexy as hell bikini. A different kind of bulge is forming, one that only deflates when I silently repeat the words, *"Mom is watching, Mom is watching,"* over and over again.

CHAPTER SEVEN

MALI

The expression on Jagger's face as I walk toward him gives me the encouragement I need. I've been standing in his bedroom for the past several minutes staring at myself in his full-length mirror. After putting on my bikini, a severe case of the doubts hit me.

There were so many women who tried to get his attention at the club. So many were better built, they were more beautiful, and they were much more experienced. I can't think of one thing I have to offer him that he can't get from a hundred other willing women.

But right now he's looking at me as if I'm the only woman alive. He makes me feel alive and gives me the courage I need to see this agreement through. I'm still shocked that I even propositioned him with this ludicrous plan, but the truth is I don't want to turn back now.

"The food is ready for the grill," Jagger says absently, as his eyes feast on me.

"I would've helped you with that, Jagger," Marlene chides him.

"It's fine, Mom," he replies then licks his lips. "Dad and Cass are already out by the pool if you want to join them."

It sounds like he wants her to join them. But I don't know if he wants me to go outside without him.

"Do you need me to help you with anything, Jagger?" I offer.

His eyes widen briefly before slightly narrowing at me. They darken from his chocolate brown to almost black and he draws in a deep breath. "Sure, if you don't mind," he huskily replies.

"Not at all," I smile as my bravado kicks in. "I'll be out in a few minutes, Marlene."

"Okay, sweetheart," she replies as she walks past Jagger toward the kitchen. "You two don't take too long."

Jagger grabs my hand and pulls me into his bedroom behind him. The door is closed, locked, and my back is up against it faster than I can process it. His mouth is instantly on mine but his touch surprises me. There's definitely an air of urgency but his kiss is deliciously tender. His tongue flicks across my lips and a moan escapes from deep inside me.

He pulls his head back and his eyes meet mine, the fire burns brightly in them. "You're already killing me in this bikini. But when you make those sounds…" His voice trails off but his body tells me everything I need to know.

My fingers grip his arms and I pull him back to me. He leans into me, pushes his whole body against mine, and claims my mouth again. His finger skims across the skin of my thigh and I have no doubt that he's about to rock my world. As his fingers keep moving up the inside of my thigh, my body begins to tremble uncontrollably. The pounding of my heart beating resonates in my ears and I'm lost in my desire.

"Jagger," a man shouts from the other side of the door. "Are you in there primping again? It's just a pool party, dude. Come on." He bangs on the door again so hard I step toward Jagger before I get knocked out.

"Give me a fucking minute, Dane," Jagger growls through the door.

The sound of Dane's footsteps disappears down the hall before I hear the sliding glass door open and close. When I raise my eyes to look at Jagger, his frustration is palpable. "Guess it's a good thing he interrupted when he did. Your family would definitely know what we're doing in here," I say with a shrug.

"They think you're my girlfriend, Mali. They don't think we're waiting for marriage," he smirks.

"No, but they would think we should wait until after the pool party," I reply.

"Give me two seconds," he shakes his head.

Then he strips right in front of me. He's completely buck-naked, shameless, and carefree. My mouth drops open in shock, my eyes bulge out, and they are trained right on his crotch as he walks to his dresser. When he turns his back to me to find his swimming trunks, he gives me a perfect view of his sexy ass.

I've just decided his family can wait.

"Jagger," a voice that sounds a lot like Tanner yells down the hall. "We're starting, Get off, get off her, and get out here."

There's another bucket of ice water to my libido. Jagger's head jerks up at the intrusion and his eyes find mine first. His expression softens when he realizes how mortified I am. He slides his shorts up his legs, quickly ties them, and jerks the door open. "Hey, dickhead," he angrily yells.

"What?" Tanner retorts.

"That was disrespectful. Apologize to her now," Jagger demands.

"To who?" Tanner sounds completely lost.

"Come here," Jagger says as he turns toward me. I step into the hall with him and reluctantly face Tanner. "To Mali. She doesn't deserve to be embarrassed like that."

"Shit, Mali. I'm sorry," Tanner apologizes. "I didn't realize you were in there. I thought Jagger had another one of his sluts here. You don't hate me now, do you?"

"No, Tanner, I don't hate you," I laugh nervously. I don't have an excuse for why I was in Jagger's bedroom with him, with the door locked, while everyone else was outside. I'm about to be labeled as one of Jagger's sluts. "It's all good."

"Are Vince and Jennifer here? I didn't see their car," Tanner replies, confused again. Realization dawns on his face and his eyes dart between Jagger and me.

"No, I haven't talked to them today," I reply.

"Mali was listening to our demo, Tanner," Jagger lies. "She thinks her dad may be interested in hearing our music."

"That's awesome," Tanner exclaims as he forgets about his previous thoughts.

"I can't make any promises, but he'll definitely listen. The music is awesome," I smile.

"Best news I've heard all day," Tanner smiles and walks away. When he steps out on the deck, he yells the news out to the other guys. "Mali is taking our music to her dad!"

Everyone is excited and animatedly talking about the news when Jagger and I step outside. Tanner, Dane, and Wes each brought a date with them. Every girl is exactly Jagger's normal type and the polar opposite of me. They're tall, long-legged, perfect bodies, perfect hair, and perfectly tanned. Everything about them looks–*perfect*. They're all *oohing* and *ahhing* over the guys being discovered and complimenting me for being so nice.

Dane's date, the tall blonde with obviously fake boobs, long, muscular legs, and wearing high heels at a pool party, struts up to Jagger and smirks at him. "You'll finally be able to achieve your lifelong goal of dating a *Victoria's Secret* model then, Jagger."

"Why would he do that?" Marlene asks defensively. "Mali is already his girlfriend."

All heads jerk toward me. The three model-esque statues, along with the other members of the band, examine me like an insect under a microscope. The blonde beside

78

Jagger snarls her lip in obvious disgust as she swings her gaze back to Jagger.

"You told me you don't have girlfriends, Jagger," she says accusingly. "You blow me off and pick *her* over *me*?"

"Girlfriend?" Tanner asks, trying to catch up in the conversation. "What the hell is going on, Jagger?"

Dwayne steps forward. "That's right, he did choose Mali. Jagger told us himself. Aren't you going to defend your girlfriend, son?"

"Can everyone calm the fuck down?" Jagger yells. He directs his anger toward the blonde first. "My personal life is none of your business and I don't owe you any explanation. You're here with Dane, in case you forgot, so I suggest you get back over there with him.

"And Tanner, we're brothers, we're best friends, but you're the last person I'd take advice from about women. Stand down now before you piss me off.

"This is a pool party, a family and friends get together, and there's plenty of food and beer. Anyone who wants to start stupid shit can leave now. Otherwise, let's get back to the good news and have some fun together," Jagger demands.

The momentary excitement dissipates and everyone returns to what they were doing before all hell broke loose. As much as this scene bothers me, I'm glad it happened. One thing I can say about myself is that I learn quickly. Now I know exactly what I have to do.

"You ready for a swim?" Jagger asks as he puts his arm around my waist. When he's close enough to whisper, he asks the question he really wants to know. "Are you okay?"

"Yeah, a swim sounds great," I smile like nothing bothers me.

When I step out of his embrace, I see the blonde watching us with obvious envy. She's stretched out on a lounge chair, rubbing sunscreen on her skin. She obviously doesn't want to get her hair wet. Or maybe she's afraid she'll melt like a wicked witch if the water hits her. I walk to the diving board and perfectly execute a forward one-and-a-half somersault straight dive.

When I surface, I have to quickly turn my face away from her shocked expression before I burst out in laughter. It's a mixture of amazement, disgust, and envy with a lot of surprise. There's one thing I'm better at than she is. Dwayne, Marlene, and Cass all stand and cheer for me as I exit the pool.

The water drips off of me in small rivers as I haul myself up the ladder in the deep end. Jagger quickly walks to me, his expression relaying his surprise that quickly morphs into fascination. He takes my hand and walks me out of earshot of the others. "That was amazing, Mali," he commends. "I had no idea you could do that."

"That's why I'm only here for a little while," I admit. "I'm in training and have Olympic try-outs at the end of the summer."

"I'm obviously no expert, but I don't see how you wouldn't make it with that dive," he says sincerely.

I smile and shake my head. "That's not even close to the hardest dive, Jagger. But thank you for the compliment anyway. It means a lot to me."

"Is this what you spend all your time doing? Diving, practicing dives, learning new dives?"

"Yes, I spend every spare second on the springboard or the platform. There's not a lot of time left to date when you're going for the gold," I explain.

"You keep surprising me. Every time I think I have you figured out, you throw something else at me that trips me up," he replies, with admiration thick in his tone.

I'm not sure how to respond to that, but I feel something deeper pass between us for the few seconds that we stare into each other's eyes. I'm not so foolish as to think this is love. But it does feel like a deeper level of respect, and the intense desire is also definitely still there.

Wes turns the outdoor stereo on and the sounds of Jagger York, the band, flow through the speakers. When his voice fills the air with a sultry slow song about wanting someone he can't have, the words suddenly seem too personal, too fitting for our situation. I quickly look away and break the spell that he has cast over me.

"I'd like to get a copy of that CD today. Do you have extras here?" I ask without looking at him.

The change in his tone is obvious and so is the punctuated pause he takes before he answers me. "Yeah, I have a couple of them here. Why do you need it today?"

"Just to have," I reply as vaguely as possible.

Before he can protest, Marlene and Cass approach us. "We need to get the grill going if we plan to eat soon," Marlene takes charge.

"Okay, Mom. I'll light it," Jagger answers her. But from the corner of my eye, I see that he's still looking at me.

When he takes a step toward the grill and is preoccupied with his mom, I take the opportunity I need. "Jagger, where is that CD? I'll grab it and put it in my purse so I don't forget."

He's knelt down with his head underneath the grill as he turns on the propane tank. He stops, cuts his eyes to me, and I see the wheels turning in his mind. "They're in the den, in the storage underneath the TV. No need to rush to get it, though."

"What do you mean 'no rush'?" Tanner asks. "Of course there's a rush. The sooner the better."

"I just meant she doesn't have to rush inside to get it right now," Jagger hedges.

"If there's a possibility that she'll forget it later, let her go get it now. Where's the harm in that? She's just looking out for us," Tanner argues. "Why are you acting so strange today?"

"I'm not acting strange. Shut the fuck up. I'm just saying she can stay outside with us and enjoy the party," Jagger explains. He keeps cutting his eyes over to me and I see the warning in them. He obviously thinks I'm up to something.

While Tanner questions Jagger further, I silently walk away from the pool party. Once inside, I quickly grab my clothes from Jagger's bedroom and peek outside. Something's not working on the grill and he has a yard full of hungry people holding his attention. The CDs are exactly where he said they were. I grab one, walk out the front door, and hop in my car to drive back to my condo alone.

I don't belong in this world. In his world. The pangs of jealousy I felt when the blonde bimbo insinuated she'd been with Jagger are proof that this will end badly for me. Inwardly, I berate myself for my own foolishness. My wish to try something new, live a little while I'm young enough, and walk on the wild side is apparently too far out of my element. Nothing about me is his type, I'd never measure up to the hordes of women who throw themselves at him, and I'd fall head over heels in love with his family. All of this simply means too much is at stake to carry out this foolish plan.

I know without a doubt that I'm better off without Jagger York in my life.

That's what I try to convince myself of, anyway. The squeezing that tightens in my chest with each mile that ticks off means nothing. At all.

CHAPTER EIGHT

JAGGER

"Mali," I yell before I pound on her door again. "Open this damn door right now. I will stand out here all night and keep your neighbors up if you don't let me in."

Silence. Complete silence greets me from the other side. Her car is here so I know she's here, but she's avoiding me. She left without a word and hasn't answered her phone for hours. Now she's not coming to her door. If she thinks I'm leaving without an explanation, she's crazy as hell.

"Mali, open this door," I demand.

"Jagger," she calls disbelievingly from behind me.

I whirl around, ready to raise hell with her, but she looks so tired. And so beautiful at the same time. She's wearing a one-piece bathing suit, her towel is draped around her shoulders, and her bag hangs on her shoulder. She's obviously been in the pool while I've been banging on her door.

"What are you doing here?" she asks. "Your family is in town to visit you."

"Yeah, about that. Funny thing happened to me today. I had a pool party and cookout at my house. My date, *my girlfriend*, just up and fucking disappeared on me," I growl at her.

Her eyes drop to the ground before she replies. "I'm not your girlfriend, Jagger. You don't have to pretend anymore."

"It was a little difficult to explain to my family why my girlfriend just left without a word. Without an explanation. Without a goodbye," I continue.

"I'm sorry about that. Maybe you should just tell them the truth, that I'm not your girlfriend. I shouldn't have I put you in that predicament to begin with. If you want me to, I'll explain it to them and take all the blame," she replies sadly.

"Maybe you can explain it to me first," I retort.

She inhales a ragged breath, looks around nervously, before her shoulders sag in resignation. "Come on in," she motions toward her door. "At least we can talk privately in there."

She retrieves her keys from her bag and steps toward the door. My hand reaches out, takes the keys from her, and I unlock the door but then palm her keys. If she had any plans of jumping inside and locking me out, I'm putting a stop to that right now.

Mali walks in first and I step inside behind her, then immediately lock the door. She takes her time to put her stuff down and keeps her back to me. I'm not backing down, I'm not leaving, and I'm not making this conversation easy on her.

"Jagger, you don't have to worry about me sabotaging your career. I'd never do that. My dad will get your music and I'll make sure he listens to it," she promises.

"That doesn't answer my question and you know it."

Her shoulders rise as she takes a deep breath and her ribs contract as she releases it. "It's not because of anything you did or didn't do. This arrangement just won't work, Jagger, and I just realized it today. It's best to stop it now before anything really even happens between us. It's only been one day so it shouldn't be a big deal anyway."

"Then why does it feel like you're making it a big deal?" I ask pointedly.

"I'm not making it a big deal. I quietly walked away but I'm keeping my end of the deal. You're the one who came over here to knock my door down," she replies. "I've told

88

you several times, I won't go back on my end of the bargain."

"What if I want to spend the summer with you?" I ask and surprise myself.

Her sarcastic laugh catches me off guard. She turns to look at me and I see her determination, her inner drive, kick in. "Why would you want me? I'm not your type at all. I don't fit in with your friends and their girlfriends.

"I'm not a tall cover-model goddess. I'm not experienced. I can't offer you everything those girls can. The possibility of a record deal is the only reason you agreed to a monogamous summer with me anyway," she argues.

"That's not fair. Did I compare you to those girls even once? Have I said I expected you to be experienced or give me anything you think they have?"

"No, you haven't said it, but you don't have to. It's just who you are and what you're used to. I'm not blaming you for it. Like I said, I just realized today that I can't go through with this," she replies quietly.

"Just who I am? What does that even mean?" I have a good idea of what she means, but for some reason that statement stung me to the core coming from her.

"You're the hot lead singer of an up and coming band. You're the man who has sworn off all relationships. Even the people closest to you didn't believe I could be your girlfriend. And I know I'm not, but the point is they couldn't see us together, even when you said we were, Jagger.

"And you told me that your own sister would never believe it. She never asked me about it, so my guess is she asked you and you've already explained it to her. That's why she never pushed it," she guesses. Correctly.

When I don't answer, she can't hide the disappointment from showing on her face.

"That's what I thought," she nods slowly. "Too many lines were crossed today. Lying to your parents. Telling a different story to your band. My focus has to be on my diving and your focus has to be on your music. Neither of us have time for these complications.

"I have no hard feelings against you, Jagger. You're a good guy underneath that fake *I don't give a shit* attitude. You should let your heart show more often. It's the best part of you," she says with a sad smile.

She's right on every count. This has become way too complicated. I've lied to my family. I've withheld information from my band. If things had ended badly between us, it

90

could've royally fucked up our chances of being signed by Milo Greyson, or anyone else for that matter. She's not my normal type—I never go for any girl that has so much depth to her.

So fuck if I can explain why my feet carry me across the floor. There's no viable explanation for why I wrap my arms around her, palm her ass with my hands, lift her until her legs wrap around my waist, and kiss her like a crazed man.

But there it is anyway.

I walk to the wall with her wrapped around my body. She doesn't try to hide her desire for me. She doesn't play coy and act like she doesn't know what I want. She grinds against me as my cock pushes against the inside of my shorts until it's almost painful. With her back against the wall and her body supported by my leg and my hand, I run my other hand across her peaked nipple.

Her responding moan shoots through me like a lightning bolt. Sliding my fingers up to the strap on her shoulder, I slide it down until her bare breast is fully exposed. My mouth follows the path my fingers made. My tongue glides down her neck, tasting her as I go. When I reach her nipple, I cover it with my mouth. My tongue circles the hardened tip and

I suck it farther into my mouth. Her fingers grip my flesh harder with each lap of my tongue.

When I skim my teeth across her sensitive nipple, her legs tighten around my waist and her head drops back to the wall behind her. "Mmm, Jagger," she moans.

"Where is your bedroom?" I ask in between lavishing attention on her breasts.

"It's," she begins to answer but stops speaking to moan again.

"Tell me now or I'm taking you right here against this wall," I threaten.

"It's through that door." She points down the hall and I briskly walk toward it.

"Last chance to change your mind, Mali. You can't say you don't want me as much as I want you," I hurriedly state. "But if you say stop, it stops here and now."

"Don't stop, Jagger," she partially begs. "I don't want you to stop."

We reach her bed and I place her in the middle of it. With both hands free, I peel her bathing suit the rest of the way off of her. With no other clothes in the way, I can now feast on her entire body. She's perfect, with her toned swimmer's legs, taut stomach, and perky breasts.

"Fuck, Mali, your body drives me wild. I don't know where to start first. Your breasts?" I ask rhetorically as I lave one with my tongue.

"Maybe your stomach?" I move down her torso to her abdomen, leaving kisses, licks, and bites along the way.

"Do you think I should go lower?" I murmur against her skin. "I love your muscular legs. Especially your thighs."

My tongue follows directions and finds her inner thighs. I run it along the sinewy striation and her fingers rush through my hair, pulling it tightly into her fists.

"Mmm, you taste good. I bet you taste good here, too. Don't you, baby?" She bucks seductively under me when I lightly lick her clit. Her moans fill the room and her hands grip me tighter to hold me in place.

"Is this what you want, Mali?" I ask, before I finish my plan of driving her wild. My lips cover her clit and my tongue circles it several times. Her hips buck as she tries to contain her pleasure. "Don't hold back on me. This scream is mine," I demand as I alternate sucking, licking, and grating my teeth across her sex.

When her cries become louder, I slide my finger into her warm, wet channel. Slowly sliding it in and out of her, I feel her body preparing for her first orgasm. Her inner walls constrict tighter around my finger and her incoherent words spur me on. Crooking my finger inside her, I stroke the spot that completely unhinges her. She screams my name loudly and it's the most beautiful sound. Watching her come apart at the seams from my touch is the most beautiful sight. Knowing she's completely sated and unable to move a muscle after having all of her energy drained is the most satisfying feeling.

"Don't run from me again, Mali," my tone warns her. "I don't doubt that you'll keep your word to me. Stop using excuses to push me away just because you're afraid to get out of your comfort zone. I told you to make a decision and stick with it. You picked me and I'm going to hold you to it now, Wildcat."

She nods and a tear runs out of her eye, down her temple, and into her chestnut brown hair. "Why, Jagger?"

"Why what?"

"Why are you so insistent about this? I gave you an out. And you still have it, if you want it. But why do you want this part of the deal so much?" she whispers.

Her humble nature stuns me. "You really have no idea how beautiful you are, do you? You don't realize how badly I want you. You don't see that you have more grace and sex appeal in your pinky finger than all those other girls have combined. Maybe I also like spending time with you. Did you ever think about that?"

"No," she answers truthfully. "I honestly never thought you'd want to just spend time with me."

"Quit thinking so much. Don't fight it. Just let it flow easily between us. We'll both walk away with great memories, a fondness for each other, and no regrets," I urge her.

"Okay, Jagger," she half-heartedly agrees. "We'll do it your way."

I move up to hover over her beautiful body and lower my mouth to hers. Our chaste kisses feel different now. It's much more personal than it was before. It's less lustful and more affectionate. After I roll off of her and onto the bed, I pull her into my arms and listen as she fights to maintain control of her emotions.

I'm fully clothed, holding this completely naked, beautiful lady, and I've never been more fucked in my life.

CHAPTER NINE

JAGGER

Last night, I fell asleep in Mali's bed with my arms wrapped securely around her and that's exactly how I woke up. The sun is just starting to rise and I keep replaying the events of yesterday in my mind. After Mali left my place without a word, I was sure the heated argument would come to blows and an all out brawl in my backyard.

The memory of it still floods me with uncertainty...

Dane walked up to me as I traced down the problem with the grill. "What the hell is the deal, Jagger?"

"What are you talking about, Dane?" I didn't even try to hide my irritation.

"I'm talking about Mali. *Your girlfriend?* Don't pull that bullshit with me. She just up and left without saying a word to anyone. This is all going to come back and bite us in the ass, I just know it. So you need to man up and tell me what you've done."

I huffed in disgust, but I broke down and told him the truth about our relationship. Our agreement. He immediately called an emergency band member meeting, so the four of us congregated in a corner of the yard that was as far away from the others as possible.

"The idiot leader of our village has made a colossal fuck-up," Dane began. He then proceeded to explain the situation to the other guys.

"Are you fucking kidding me, Jagger?"

"What the hell were you thinking?"

"It's one thing to sink your own career, but did you have to take ours down with you?"

They all three descended on me at once. They were angrier, more disappointed, and more disgusted with me than I've ever seen them. The only thing that kept them from kicking me out of my own band was the hope that Mali could help get our music in front of her dad sooner rather than later.

"There's only one solution to this problem," Wes stated.

"What's that?" I ask dubiously.

"You have to go to her and make her keep her end of the agreement. You can't let her get away. Make her believe she's special, she's important to you, whatever the fuck you have to do just to keep her around. After Milo listens to our CD and makes his decision, you can kick her to the curb," he explained.

"Yeah, that could work," Dane agreed with Wes. "Something set her off and made her just leave out of the blue. Maybe she was pissed off after Bambi's outburst. Do you know where she lives?"

"Yes, I know where she lives. But I've made it clear to her, more than once, that I don't want her to get attached to me. This was her proposition anyway. We agreed to just one summer and then we part ways. I'm not promising her a white picket fence and a date to go pick out china patterns," I adamantly refused.

"You can play it off better than that," Tanner scolded me. "You don't have to say a word about love, or a life together, or any of that shit. You're a master manipulator when it comes to women. Shit, look at this very situation as proof. Somehow, you convinced a good girl that she was secretly bad, but you made her believe it was all her idea."

"It *was* her idea," I exclaimed. "It wasn't mine at all. She insisted on the whole monogamous summer thing. I agreed because she's hot as hell, there's a freak under that prudish exterior, and her dad can take our band to a whole new level."

"Get over there and fix this *tonight*, Jagger. I fucking mean it," Dane pressured. "I don't care if you have to promise her you'll buy her a ring for Christmas. Get her back for the summer, or long enough to get us signed, and then you can do whatever the hell you want."

"Fine. My family just got here today but I'll go over in a few hours to smooth things over with her," I agreed.

"Whatever you have to promise her to win her back," Dane reiterated.

"Don't let us down," Tanner added.

"Yeah, yeah, I got it," I dismissed them.

When I finally got the grill going, I was absently poking the chicken with the long-handled fork when my dad walked up beside me.

"Where'd Mali go?" he asked.

"I think she got upset over what Dane's date, Bambi, said. She went home," I replied.

He nodded slowly. "Mali's a keeper, Jagger. I know it's only been a day, but anyone can see she's a caring person."

"What do you mean 'it's only been a day'?" I asked, stunned that he knew that. I thought I'd have to kill Cass for running her mouth.

"I've only known her for a day," he replied as he leveled me with his gaze. "What did you think I meant?"

"I thought you were talking about me," I answered truthfully.

"Now that you mention it, you do act like you just met her yesterday," Dad mused.

"Huh?" I asked.

He laughed at my confusion. Or my panic that he knew the truth. Either one. "If you can't see what you have in her, then you must have just met her yesterday and you're still too blind to see it. You'd be a total fool to let that one get away, son."

"My band mates just ordered me to go to her place tonight and get her back," I admitted. "I'm torn over it, honestly."

"Our therapist put it in simple terms for your mom and me when we were having problems," Dad said. "Picture yourself doing what you love the most, like your music, for example. If you can see yourself being happy without having her by your side when you travel around the country, sing to thousands of people, and sign autographs, then let her go.

"But if you can't stand the thought of her doing all those things at another man's side, you'll be sorry you let her go. Just know if you do let her go, you may not ever get her back again," he concluded.

So I'm here in her luxury condo after bribing the security guard to let me back in the gated community. She's lying in my arms after I convinced her it's best that we continue this crazy charade. All I can do is take this charade one day at a time. I'll try to keep things light between us, but also keep her interested enough to hang out with me all summer.

When Mali shifts in her sleep, her long hair falls away from her shoulder and gives me an unobstructed view of her beautiful face. She looks so peaceful in her sleep. Her lips twitch before turning upward into a shy smile. She's definitely dreaming from the way her eyes dart in all directions underneath her eyelids.

I can't resist leaning in to kiss her eyes in her sleep. She stirs a little, her eyes flutter, and then she sleepily opens them. "Mmm…it's too early. Go back to sleep," she slurs.

"Not ready to face the day, sleepyhead?" I tease.

"Nuh uh," she mutters. "You feel too good. Hold me."

I can't help but smile at how adorable she is, even when she's asleep. Never in a million years would I ever admit that I secretly like this–having someone to hold, to actually sleep with, and to wake up with. My dad's words ring in my ears.

Mali's right. It's way too early for this shit. Sliding back into position, I pull her close to me and close my eyes. Her warm body is pressed against mine. Her soft sighs of contentment fly straight through me. There's no way she doesn't feel my morning wood as it grows against her ass. It's fucking killing me to be this close and not seal the deal. Our arrangement needs to hit fast forward before they're permanently blue.

The last thought I have before I drift off to sleep concerns me, though. *Would it bother me if another man held Mali while she slept?*

MALI

Whose arms are wrapped around me?

Not so much fun when that's my first thought of the day. Memories of last night resurface and I can't stop the smile that covers my face. I'd all but given up on anything remotely associated with Jagger York. Then he showed up at my condo, loudly pounded on my door, and demanded I let him in.

I ran when I realized I didn't belong in his world, around all those beautiful people. When that blonde bitch went out of her way to say she'd had sex with Jagger before, it really knocked the wind out of my sails. Her sole purpose in her words was to tell me I couldn't measure up to her.

It was childish to retaliate like I did, but I had to show her that she couldn't compete with me. The dive I chose to do was actually fairly difficult. But with Jagger bragging on me and openly showing he was impressed, I wanted to play it off in front of her. Regardless, it worked and it pissed her off.

Jagger did the very thing I never thought he would do. He chased me down and insisted we keep seeing each other. If I keep analyzing why I think he did it, what he's really thinking, and what this means in the long run, I'll drive myself crazy. The best I can hope for is just what he said about having fun, great memories, and an easy parting.

It'll be easy for him anyway. I'm not the casual relationship kind of girl. When I start seeing someone, it's usually because I'm interested in the guy and can see us having a long-term relationship. Jagger felt different, more dangerous, and more exciting from the beginning. The problem is, the more time I spend with him, the more things I find I genuinely like about him.

Letting go of him after a few months of this won't be so easy. That's why I went to the pool and practiced for several hours yesterday. I punished my body to the point of exhaustion so I could hopefully fall asleep without thinking about him. He had better ways of wearing me out though.

"I know you're awake, Wildcat," he says from behind me, his voice still groggy with sleep. "The wheels are turning so loudly in your head they woke me up."

Playfully, I elbow him in the ribs and chuckle. "Shut up. They are not. You're just one of those crazy morning people who thinks everyone else is, too."

"Are you really going to try to tell me you're not laying there overthinking everything?"

"What's there to overthink?" I retort.

"Exactly. So relax," he replies.

"I'm laying in my bed, barely even awake, Jagger. I can't get much more relaxed than this."

"If you say so," he chuckles. "I'm going to head home now and start getting today's grilling menu prepared. Come on over when you get up. Wear your bathing suit again. I really liked that bikini you wore yesterday. You looked so sexy in it."

"Okay," I agree. "I'll be there, ready to swim again. Will everyone else be there again today?"

"Yeah," he answers reluctantly. "If Bambi gives you a hard time, I'll tell Dane not to bring her again."

"Bambi? That's really her name?" I rise up on one arm and turn to look at him. *Is he joking?* "No wonder she's as dumb as a box of rocks. She must have screwed her teachers just to graduate high school."

Jagger laughs lightly at first then breaks into a fit of laughter. "You're probably right. I never thought of it like that."

Our laughter fades but our eyes remain locked. Unspoken words hang in the air between us. I only wish I knew what his were.

"Okay then," he says, breaking the spell. "I need to get going." He stands, dresses, and walks toward the door. Before he walks through the doorway, he stops, turns, and pins me with his serious expression. "Don't make me have to come find you."

"And if I do?" I mockingly call his bluff.

His eyes instantly become heated as the sexy smirk takes over his face. He takes slow, deliberate steps back toward me. "Mali," he lowers his head as he speaks. "If I have to come after you one more time, I'll bend you over," he intentionally pauses, "my knee. Then I'll spank that luscious ass until you're desperately begging me."

"That's not very much incentive for me to show up, is it?" I slowly lift one eyebrow as I challenge him.

He laughs, but it's an evil genius type of laugh that sends shivers through me. "You'll be desperately begging me to make you come, Wildcat, because I'll keep you right on the edge for hours. If you show up on your own, I'll make sure you repeatedly come. Your choice."

"I'll be there," I quickly concur.

"You better be," he leans in and kisses me goodbye. "I have big plans to start your *let loose and have fun* training."

Is this where I should be more careful what I wish for?

When I arrive at his house after taking my time to get dressed, the pool party is in full swing. The band members are here with their dates, including Bimbo, along with Jagger's family. I wore my bathing suit under a simple cover-up this time, so I walked straight out to the back deck.

Jagger sees me from across the pool the second I enter his back yard and struts over to me. He wraps his arms around my waist, pulls me to him, and thoroughly kisses me in front of everyone. My body becomes like putty in his hands, molding and shaping to fit his body.

"There's my girl," he murmurs against my lips. "You'll be so very thankful you showed up when I get you alone tonight."

"I'll hold you to that promise," I flirt.

Bimbo approaches the diving board and cuts her eyes menacingly over at me. She waits for Jagger to finally look at her before she moves to the end of the board. She's apparently watched a few YouTube videos as she begins to bounce up and down, gaining height. Her fake boobs are flopping so hard I'm waiting to see her with two black eyes. She pulls her right leg up to a ninety-degree angle, points her foot, and uses her arms to propel herself even higher.

Just as she's about to execute her dive of choice, she loses her balance on the wet springboard. Her foot slides out of from underneath her and she crashes down to the board on her ass. Then she topples over, rather ungracefully, and ends up doing a complete belly flop into the water.

Everyone else surrounding the pool stands and laughingly cheers. But I can no longer hold back my own cackle when Jagger looks at me and asks, "Is that a new dive you need to know about?"

"Yeah, the Bimbo Belly Flop," I reply.

She sputters to the side of the pool, her face red with embarrassment and her stomach red with stinging from the water, but nothing is hurt other than her pride. She stomps back to her lounge chair, puts on her sunglasses, and sears me with her angry stare.

When everyone starts to leave, I collect my things and walk toward the front door, too. Jagger gives me his *what the hell* look and wraps his hand around mine.

"Where do you think you're going?" he asks.

"I didn't bring anything to spend the night, Jagger. Everything I need for tomorrow is back at my condo. I should really go home tonight," I explain.

He reluctantly lets me go, knowing my week days are hard enough without getting up even earlier to swing by my place first. After a long, scorching kiss, followed by an impromptu make-out session inside my car, I'm finally on my way back to my place.

CHAPTER TEN

JAGGER

JULY

After two weeks of only texting and talking on the phone daily, I've been dying to see Mali again. She had to leave Miami for several days during the week, so her dive coach made her practice on the following two weekends as punishment. Okay, fine, it was punishment for me and valuable practice time for her, but I still pouted like a little kid over it.

Mali said I was adorable when I didn't get my way.

I convinced her to come to my house for a while after practice tonight. It wasn't easy, but she said she'd be here. As soon as she pulls in the driveway, I'm out the door and opening her car door for her. I take her offered hand and pull her out of the car, and straight into my embrace.

"It's good to see you, too, Jagger," she chuckles. "I'm sorry but I can only stay about an hour."

"That's not nearly long enough but I'll take it. It's better than nothing," I reply. "No more leaving town and missing practice."

"Deal," she agrees.

For my hour-long conjugal visit with her, I decide to do something extremely out of character. I lead her to the lounge chairs on the back deck, have her lie back, and then I squeeze in beside her in the same chair. The whole sixty minutes are spent just talking about any and everything. It's by far the best conversation I've ever had. My family really needs to find somewhere else to live as soon as possible. It's not that I don't love them, but I really need time alone with Mali and I feel like I'm constantly ditching them when they're my guests.

It sucks.

What sucks even worse is my hour is up and Mali says she has to go home.

"It's time to start your training," I state as we walk out together. "I've been slacking."

"Sounds good. What's the plan?" she asks enthusiastically.

"Friday night, you're going to meet me at The Vine Room," I instruct her.

"Fancy," she replies. "Very upscale jazz club."

"Exactly. Look the part. We're starting with the art of seduction," I explain.

"Sounds fun," she purrs. "Are you going to seduce me, Jagger?"

"No, Mali. You're going to seduce me," I correct her.

"What?" she stammers. "Wait a minute. You want me to pick you up in a bar?"

"Exactly," I nod. "But not in a nightclub when you're brave after a few drinks. In a jazz club when you're sober and confident."

She sounds unsure but she agrees anyway. "Okay, I'll be there."

"Eight o'clock. Don't be late," I adamantly state.

"You're sure about this?" she asks tentatively.

"I'm positive. You'll enjoy it," I reassure her.

Before she can protest further, I lean in to kiss her, shut her car door, and wave goodbye as I walk backward to my house.

"Where's Mali going?" Dad asks, surprising me.

"She's going back to her place," I reply as I walk past him.

"I'm surprised she's not staying here with you," he continues.

111

"We're not living together, Dad. We just recently agreed to be exclusive," I stop and face him. "Don't want to get on each other's nerves already."

"I didn't say anything about living together. We just haven't had much time alone with her, though," Dad replies.

"We both have things we have to do during the week. I have guitar lessons to give at the studio and she has dive practice every day. I'm meeting her out this Friday night."

"Your mom and I are going to look at a couple of houses this week. Wish us luck," he says, abruptly changing the subject.

"Take your time," I answer, like a good son. "No need to rush off."

After getting through no less than four sleepless nights, it's finally Friday. I'm in the kitchen making coffee when Cass comes shuffling in like a zombie from *The Walking Dead*. She yawns with a loud, hurt animal sound and rubs the sleep from her eyes.

"You look like shit," I laugh.

"You don't look so hot yourself, big brother," she punches me in the arm. "Why do you look like you pulled another all-nighter?"

"I just haven't slept very well," I reply and look away.

"Huh. Couldn't sleep or couldn't stop dreaming?" she narrows her eyes at me.

My head jerks in her direction and I stare at her as I try to determine what she knows.

"You still talk in your sleep, Jagger," Cass laughs her evil laugh. "So, who took Mali away from you?"

"What?" I ask as I search my memory. Yeah, I dreamed about Mali all night. Again. One dream led to another one and I woke up every night at least a million times.

"You said 'I can't lose her,' very clearly," Cass relayed.

"I don't remember that. How do you know I meant Mali?"

"You said her name before that, but you mumbled so I couldn't make out what you said."

"Why are you stalking me in my sleep? That's weird. Really weird," I chastise her and pour her coffee.

"Whatever, big bro. You were loud and woke me up. When I wake up, I have to get up and pee. Keep your trap shut tonight and we won't have this problem again," Cass says as she takes her coffee mug to the table.

An hour later, I've showered, drank enough coffee to bathe in, and I'm walking out the door for work. I give guitar lessons to aspiring musicians at a high-end music store. Translation: I teach spoiled brats, whose parents pawn them off on me to babysit, how to play the guitar. They then go home and drive their parents crazy with their inability to play anything remotely coherent.

I get paid well enough for it and I actually do love it, especially with the people who are a natural. Watching their talent develop is the best. But today my mind keeps wandering to a certain little brunette who is supposed to rock my world tonight.

While the current client plays his practice chords, I pull out my phone and send her a naughty text. I know she's in the water today so it'll be a while before she can answer, but at least it'll be waiting for her. We've texted every night and she's gotten a little braver with each conversation. I'm slowly winning her over to the dark side.

IOU several orgasms. Didn't keep my promise the other night.

The three little dots show on my screen, showing me she's typing a reply back to me.

"What are you smiling about? Am I doing good?" the kid asks me.

"Um, yeah, you're doing great. Keep going," I tell him.

Mali: You get one pass. Only bc I feel bad you haven't had your first one yet. After that, all bets are off.

Me: We can always skip the jazz club.

Mali: No way. Already picked out my outfit.

Me: Are you texting wet?

The three dots show, then disappear. Then show. Then disappear. Now they're back again.

Mali: Oh, I'm wet. But I haven't been in the pool yet.

"Ah, shit," I exclaim. The kid beside me nearly jumps out of his chair.

"Did I do something wrong?"

"No, man. I just remembered something I was supposed to do," I lie. "Keep going."

Me: You made me say a bad word. I'm collecting my due tonight.

Mali: You're sure playing hard to get. LOL

Me: You'll see hard tonight all right.

Mali: Promises. Time for my total body lubricant. TTYL

Shit. Now I can't wait for this day to be over with so I can see her again. It's been a long week of cold showers and not seeing her while I spent time with my family.

Her practice schedule is grueling and she's usually worn out at the end of the day. My band practices at night and we play at the nightclub Tuesday, Thursday, and Saturday nights. Our schedule makes it difficult to spend much time together during the week. Still, every night after our ritual texts, I consider just showing up at her condo.

Finally, after endless hours of listening to others mutilate the sweet sounds the guitar is designed to make, it's time to leave and meet Mali. I hurry home, shower, change clothes, and rush toward the front door.

"Going to see Mali?" Mom asks.

"Yeah, sorry to run out on you again," I apologize.

"No need to be sorry. Go finish falling in love with her," she urges.

"Mom," I groan. "I'm not in love with her."

"Jagger, I'm your mom. I raised you. You can't always see the truth about yourself. Stop fighting it and just let it happen. It's easy," she advises. "What are you waiting for?"

"I don't know, Mom," I admit. "I don't know that I'm waiting for anything. I like spending time with her. It's not love though."

"Don't wait so long to realize it that she moves on without you. You'll always think of

116

her as the one that got away then," Mom replies. Her voice is full of sympathy, like it's already happened.

Her words stay with me all the way to The Vine Room. She thinks I'm in love with Mali after a few weeks of pretend dating. That's ludicrous. I arrive at the club ten minutes early. Perfect for me to have a drink before she gets here. I choose a booth that's private and in the shadows of the low lighting.

I'm sipping on a tumbler of bourbon when the air around me sparks with electricity. She's here. I feel her before I see her. My eyes scan the room, looking for the source of my increased heart rate. What the hell is wrong with me? I never get worked up over a girl.

It's from going so long without sex. That's what makes a sane man lose his shit, walk down the aisle to say I do, and give up exciting and gratifying sex for the rest of his life. Just the prospect of having sex again after an extended dry spell can make a man do something completely stupid. That'll never be me.

And there she is.

I'm not that guy. The man who'll promise her the fucking moon and stars for all eternity in return for one night of unbridled passion. See my point? Who the fuck thinks 'unbridled passion' in this generation? To keep my man-card, I have to amend that thought. She can have every fucking star in the sky if I can fuck her fifty ways to Sunday all in one night. This very night. Tonight.

I thought she'd be nervous when she walked in a strange place alone. She's actually just the opposite. She's confident, poised, and so fucking beautiful my chest hurts from the squeezing sensation. Maybe the pain is from a lack of air since my brain has forgotten to tell my body to breathe.

Another man approaches her, obviously flirting with her, and offers to buy her a drink and I'm instantly on alert. Her warm smile lights up her face as she lets him down easy. He mutters something about a 'lucky fucking bastard' as he turns away from her. *That's me he's referring to*, I think smugly. When her eyes land on mine, I feel the arc of electricity pass between us but she's definitely the one in charge tonight.

Her hips sway seductively in her little black dress as she walks directly to me. *To me.* Not the vacant side of the booth. She bends at the waist and the plunging V of her dress gapes open, giving me an unobstructed view and an uncontrollable salivation problem. Her soft lips land on mine and I use all of my might to not throw her on the table when her tongue lightly licks across my lips.

Shit, I'm ready to leave right now. Fuck the rest of her seduction lesson. Fuck the small talk, dinner, and drinks. Fuck her the rest of the night, that's all I want to do.

"Hello, Jagger," her voice hums seductively. "I've missed that so much."

"What?" I intelligently reply.

"Your kiss." She smiles as she swipes her thumb across my lips to wipe her lipstick off me.

I grab her wrist to stop her. "I didn't get enough," I say as I pull her to me and bury my tongue in her mouth. She responds in kind and before long I hear uncomfortable laughs around us. They remind me I'm in a public place thinking about doing very private things.

"You've missed me," she smiles and slides into the booth seat beside me.

"You look beautiful tonight," I compliment her and avoid admitting the obvious. Her smile falters for a split second and I feel like shit. Then I remind myself what this really is between us. Repeatedly remind myself.

"Thank you. You look very handsome, Jagger," she looks at me admiringly. "What are you having?"

"Bourbon. Would you like me to order you one?"

"I remember the last time you ordered a drink for me. Maybe I should order this one," she laughs. "But then again, I haven't forgotten that you owe me several screaming orgasms."

She laid that on me just as I took a sip of my drink. After my sputtering and coughing fit, I collect myself and wrap my arm around her shoulders. I lean in close to whisper in her ear, "I haven't forgotten either. Would you like your first one right now?"

I trail my fingertips up her bare thigh to the hem of her dress. Chills fan out across her skin like ripples in water. Her chest rises and falls in quick succession as her desire takes a toll on her. My hand inches up, barely brushing the sensitive skin of her upper thigh as she inhales a deep breath.

"I'm supposed to seduce you, remember? Not the other way around," she says breathlessly. She covers my hand with hers and effectively halts my progress.

"I definitely remember," I reply. "Seems I let go of my self-control when I'm around you. I give in to demands that are completely against my character. I agree to your crazy requests, against my better judgment."

120

I'm obviously losing my touch because she took that statement completely wrong. I see it in her face, I feel it in the tenseness of her body, and I sense it in her mood change.

"Jagger," her eyebrows draw downward as her eyes dart between mine, "at any time you want out of this, all I ask is you tell me before you're with someone else. If this time apart made you regret your decision, we'll stop now."

She picks up her small purse from the table and begins to slide out of the booth. This is my chance to walk away clean before my judgment is further clouded. Snuggling with her in her apartment, our daily texts, spending non-intercourse related time with her, and thinking about her at odd times of the day–all of this is foreign to me.

She slowly stands and the conversation with my band springs to my mind. If Milo doesn't sign us, they'll blame me for letting her go. They'll say he took his revenge out on us for his daughter's broken heart. While I seriously don't think Mali is capable of doing that to us, Milo definitely is and would do it in a heartbeat.

"Mali," I call to her and she stops. "I did miss you this week. And the past two weeks."

The hopeful expression in her eyes kills me. Cass was right when she said Mali couldn't do this without becoming attached to me. I'm such a shithead.

Disbelief clouds her eyes, replacing the hope that was just there. "You missed me?"

She doesn't sound convinced.

"I did," I nod. "And I didn't mean that the way it sounded. I meant your persuasion skills are already pretty effective. When I said you make me lose my self-control and get me to agree to things, that was a compliment to you. Not many people can make those claims."

She takes her seat again but the playful, affectionate Mali is gone. All-business Mali has taken her place. "By all means then, finish what you started," she challenges.

She's purposely distancing herself from me.

I'm already losing her.

"Mali," I say, my tone both a warning and a plea.

"Maybe what you said earlier today was spot on," she replies, ignoring my unspoken request.

"What's that?"

"We should skip the jazz club. Let's go to my place now."

Without waiting for my reply, she grabs her purse, suddenly stands, and quickly walks out the door. I throw a few bills on the table to cover my tab and follow her outside. I step outside the club just in time to see her car pull away from the curb.

She stops when she sees me. "I'll tell the guard to expect you."

CHAPTER ELEVEN
MALI

"I must be the dumbest person on Earth." I strike the steering wheel in anger with the side of my fist. "I knew better. This was my fucking idea. It's not fair for me to be disappointed in him."

I openly talk to myself even more as my foot presses harder on the accelerator, propelling me faster and faster toward the condo. Now I feel like an idiot for causing a scene at the club and I want to make it up to him.

I'm going to blame my outburst on sexual frustration. He's supposed to help me shed my inhibitions like the one-night stand sleazebag Jennifer said he is. He slept with me–and literally only slept all night. He's been sweet, attentive, and affectionate. Then he's a jerk, distant, and crass. It's like every step forward we take sends us back two.

Now that I know what I need to do, and I have a somewhat of a plan forming, I've decided to take matters into my own hands.

Maybe this was part of his plan all along-drive me crazy with sexual frustration until I snap.

"Well, game on, Jagger. Bring your first string tonight because I'm not in the mood for bench warmers."

I tell the guard that Jagger will be along in a few minutes and rush to have enough time to prepare for my idea. One way or another, we're taking the next step in this agreement. Once inside my condo, I begin stripping my clothes off and leave them lying on the floor where they land. It's a breadcrumb trail for him to find me.

After I light several candles around my bedroom, I position myself in the center of the bed and send him a quick text.

Me: Door's unlocked. Lock it when you get here.

I'm surprised when my phone pings with a text.

Him: Should I be scared?

Me: Yep, if you don't hurry your ass up here.

Him: Walking in now. Be gentle with me.

Me: Not a chance in hell.

The front door opens and I hear his chuckle as he reads my reply. At least he's not mad about my erratic behavior tonight. His laughter stops and I assume he's found the trail of my shoes, dress, panties, and bra.

"Is there a prize at the end of this treasure hunt?" he asks from the hall.

When he steps into the doorway of my bedroom, he stops in his tracks as his eyes roam over my body. He takes his time, soaking in every detail of my exposure. His white knuckles from his tight fists are the only evidence of how much he's affected.

"You tell me," I reply with a sly smile.

"Fuck yeah," he growls. "I'm confused, though. I thought you were mad at me."

He slowly moves toward me, still feasting on me with his eyes.

"Not mad."

"Then what?"

Now his knee is propped on the end of the bed.

"Frustrated."

"What did I do?" he absently asks as he kicks off his shoes.

"It's what you haven't done. It's time to deliver on the many screaming orgasms you owe me."

As he crawls up my body, he positions his arms and legs on either side of me. He lightly brushes his nose and lips against my skin starting at the top of my foot, up my leg, and then lingers at my hip. The anticipation of where he'll go next kills me. He continues up my stomach, across my breast, and stops at my mouth.

"I've memorized the scent and the feel of your skin. Fantasized about licking every inch of you. Thought about you being alone in this bed when I could've been here with you. *Every fucking night this week.*"

"I hoped you would just show up," I confess.

"I'm here now, and you're mine all night. No fucking interruptions."

His possessive growl sends shivers down my spine and thrills me. Every nerve is firing on double time, making my skin ultra-sensitive to his touch. His head dips down and his mouth lands on my neck. The feel of his velvety soft tongue as he licks and sucks on me is exquisite.

He's way overdressed for this part of the evening, and I desperately want to help him remedy the problem. I fumble around to unbutton his shirt and pull it free of where it's tucked into his pants. When he shrugs out of it, I quickly unbuckle his belt, unbutton his pants, and lower his zipper.

"Take these off," I murmur against his lips.

He jumps up to step out of his pants and his boxer briefs. His cock stands proudly before me, long, thick, and hard. His hand lifts and wraps around the base and he unhurriedly slides it upward. My eyes unconsciously follow his movement, my lips part, and my breaths come in needy pants.

When his hand halts, I drag my eyes up his perfectly built body until I meet his licentious gaze. "Like what you see?"

"Definitely love what I see. Just wish it was closer to me."

"Your wish is my command, Wildcat."

He grabs a condom from his wallet, slides it on, and climbs on the bed. As he moves up my body this time, he stops at my core and raises his eyes to mine in the most seductive way. While I'm held captive by his eyes, his tongue erotically emerges as he licks my clit. My head drops back as my body convulses from the pleasure he gives me. The combination of his warm, wet tongue and the stimulation of his finger inside me has me seeing stars as I scream his name.

"Mmmm, you taste good." He kisses the inside of my thigh and I realize I'm still pulling his hair. "But I don't think I can wait one more second to be inside you, Mali."

"I can't wait another second either, Jagger."

He pushes forward on his knees and I feel his cock stroke against me. The instant we become as one, joined in beautiful decadence, something changes. A switch instantly flips and we move together in perfection. Jagger kisses me again, his tongue caresses mine, and he thrusts harder into me. My hips rise to meet his over and over. Not that I have many lovers to compare him to, but I can't imagine another could ever command my body the way Jagger does.

"I feel your body tightening around me. It's holding onto me like you can't get enough," he murmurs to me.

"I can't get enough of you, Jagger."

"I've wanted you since the second I first saw you."

"You have me," I tell him.

For a moment suspended in time, he slows his movements, gazes deeply into my eyes, and something more meaningful than sex passes between us. He'll deny it, he'll run from it, and he'll still walk away from me in the end. But it's there regardless.

His speed increases and the intense sensation multiplies, bringing me closer and closer to the pinnacle of our pleasure. My fingers dig into his shoulders as I hold on to this moment as long as I can. I'm no longer able to control my body's reaction and Jagger completely finishes me as I cry out his name. He immediately follows as he holds himself as deep inside of me as he can get.

His muscles relax and his body collapses on top of mine, totally spent. When he turns his head and sweetly kisses my cheek, his lips linger a little longer than necessary. Of all the intimate acts we've experienced tonight, that single kiss affects me the most. I'm doing the very thing I said I wouldn't do.

I'm falling for Jagger York.

I *have* to end this. How many times have I told myself that?

He slides off of me and goes straight to the bathroom. While he's cleaning up, I throw on a pair of pajamas, straighten the covers, and grab a couple of bottled waters from the refrigerator. When I walk back into my bedroom, Jagger is waiting for me in the bed.

"You're dressed." He sounds disappointed.

"I brought you a water. Thirsty?" I hand him the bottle and ignore his observation.

"Sure. I need to rehydrate for round two," he smirks.

Maybe I should wait and end this after the weekend is over.

"Only if you insist," I quip.

"Actually, I do insist. I'm kind of feeling like I'm the girl here and you're the one who's about to send me packing."

I laugh nervously. Am I that transparent?

"What the fuck, Mali? You *were* planning to," he accuses.

"I don't want you to leave, Jagger," I say sincerely, truthfully. I don't want him to go. I don't want this to end, but that's exactly why it has to. My answer satisfies him for now and he tugs on my arm to pull me into bed with him.

"You better be glad you said that," he says as he drapes his arm over me. "You're spending the whole weekend with me. No dive practice. We have to play at the club Saturday night and I want you there with me."

"Okay," I agree.

My heart hurts and is full at the same time. I'm excited about having the weekend with him, spending time with him, and just having fun together. But my heart breaks in two just knowing that when this weekend ends, so do we. I finally fall asleep wrapped protectively in his embrace.

Jagger wakes me up in the middle of the night as he removes my clothes. His mouth and hands worship my body, giving me more pleasure than I've ever had. Rolling him over on his back, I give him every ounce of love in me.

These are the memories I want to keep with me–the times when his guard is down and I see glimpses of the real Jagger. Not the public persona, but the man with a hint of vulnerability in his eyes. My eyes, hands, and mouth roam over his body, searing the vision of it firmly in my mind. His moans of pleasure when I take him fully into my mouth spur me on. His hands cover my head, tighten in my hair as his climax builds, and I don't stop until I've taken every last drop from him.

I can't help but wonder if he senses the change in me when he suddenly sits straight up. His hands cup my face. The beam of moonlight streaming in through the window is our only light, but I can clearly see his face, as if we were in broad daylight. He searches my face and my eyes, shakes his head from side to side, and furrows his brows.

"What is it, Jagger?" I ask, trying to act normal.

"Nothing," he replies. "Let's go back to sleep."

132

"Time to wake up," Jagger says as he drags his fingertips across my eyelids.

"You're way too cheerful early in the morning," I grumble.

He laughs. "Babe, it's not early in the morning. It's past eleven."

I open one eye to peek at him. "Are you serious?"

"Yep. We should already be at my house, firing up the grill and getting the food ready to cook. Everyone will be there soon and my poor parents will be there to chaperone alone."

"Okay, I'll get up. But only because your parents are great," I concede. "Is Bimbo coming over today?"

"No, Dane dumped her this week."

"Really? Why?"

He shrugs one shoulder and looks away. "He's not into relationships. She's not the type of girl any guy would get serious about anyway."

"What type is that?" I ask defensively.

"You know, the kind that screws more frequently than a Phillips head screwdriver."

"That's not fair," I retort. "He's probably worse about hopping from bed to bed than she is."

"She knew what she was getting into, Mali. He only wanted to use her for sex and he didn't hide it from her. She chose to accept it, so she can't blame him," he reasoned.

It's ironic how much the one I refer to as Bimbo sounds like me in our current arrangement.

"I'd better get in the shower so we can get to your house before everyone else."

"I'll join you." He wiggles his eyebrows suggestively and jumps off the bed. I guess that would be the green thing to do.

CHAPTER TWELVE

MALI

After our forty-five minute shower, we're finally on our way to Jagger's house for another day by the pool with his family and friends. His mom greets us as we walk in the door.

"Mali, I'm so glad you came today." She pulls me into a warm embrace. "Dwayne and I have told Jagger all week to bring you back."

"My weeks are pretty full," I explain. "I practice diving and exercise every day. There's not a lot of down time when you're training for the Olympic preliminaries."

"I guess not," she replies. "It's very impressive, though."

Jagger leaves us to change into his swimming trunks, so Marlene and I take a seat to spend time just chatting. The more I get to know her, the more I love her. She asks all about my family, diving, the upcoming Olympic trials, and what it all means for my future.

Before I realize it, Jagger has already finished grilling all the food and the guys are busy eating. Marlene and I are still busy chatting, and I love every minute of it. That's how I know what's about to come next, and how I dread being the one who has to say no.

"We should go do something together one day this week," Marlene suggests, as I knew she would.

"I'll just have to see what my schedule is like," I hesitate. "Honestly, I don't normally do anything else during the week."

"Mom," Jagger calls from the doorway. "I've already told you that I don't even get to see her during the week. Both of you need to come eat before these pigs eat it all."

Marlene and I walk into the kitchen and join the conversation already in progress. Jagger comes up behind me as I'm piling food on my plate. "Sorry about that. I've tried to tell her."

"It's okay," I reply, keeping my voice low. "It's not that I don't want to do things with her. I literally can't."

"I know, babe." He kisses my cheek. "Don't sweat it."

Vince and Jennifer pick that moment to walk in and witness what our friends have suspected for the last several weeks. I haven't asked him, but I wonder if Jagger has told his band the truth about us. It's not that I'm hiding our relationship from Jennifer. But, I have been going out of my way to not tell Jennifer about it, let her see any evidence of it, or allow her to hear anything about it from anyone else.

"What the hell is this?" she blurts out.

"What?" Jagger asks, clueless.

"Why did you just kiss her?" Looking at me, she continues her rant. "Why did he just kiss you? And what are you even doing here?"

Dwayne steps around the corner and chimes in. "Why wouldn't she be here? Mali is Jagger's girlfriend. Isn't that right, son?"

Here we are, standing between one of my best friends and my–whatever he is, and we're caught red handed in our lie. I have no idea how we get out of this predicament without looking like complete morons. Clearly, I didn't think through all the complications of the revelation I had in that nightclub bathroom. Actually, it seems fitting now that we're in deep shit between our friends and family.

Jagger looks at me thoughtfully before he answers. His expression changes right before my eyes. His eyes soften, his smile is warm, and his stance relaxes. My heart flutters. My stomach drops. My breath catches in my chest.

I silently will him not to make the major confession I know he's about to make. *Don't do it, Jagger. Don't.*

"Yes, she's my girlfriend," Jagger announces. His hand cups my cheek and he softly, but sensually, kisses my lips.

He pulls his face back to look at me, but keeps his hand on my face. His thumb tenderly strokes my cheek as he searches my eyes for confirmation. This feels so real, too real, and I can't stop how he affects me. For several seconds, I get lost in the chocolate brown depths of his eyes, where the occasional green speckle sparkles when the light hits it just right.

Then the comments that erupt in the kitchen draw me out of Jagger's trance. Dwayne and Marlene cheer loudly, loudly voicing their approval. Jennifer moved past her stunned phase and now insists I have lost my mind. Vince tries to calm Jennifer but she can't hear him over her own aggravation. Jagger's band members all give their approval.

Jagger turns from me, his amusement evident in his expression and voice, and addresses the room. "Can everyone shut the hell up? Since when is my love life any of your business?" Replies fly from everyone and

Jagger steps away from me to actively engage further.

As I glance around the boisterous room, I realize only one person hasn't voiced an opinion either way. Unfortunately, that's the one person who concerns me the most. Cass glares at Jagger with murderous intent. Her disgust with him is written all over her face and she makes no attempt to hide it.

She already knows about our arrangement, but she never acted upset about it before now. It can't be over the lies to his parents, because she knew that was the case from the start. What would make her suddenly change so drastically?

Cass looks around the room and I notice she gives his band members much the same look. All of them except Dane, that is. He gets a look of disappointment from Cass and he quickly looks away from her. I need to find out what the hell is going on. When Cass looks in my direction, our eyes meet and I get a very bad feeling in the pit of my stomach when her angry looks morphs into pity.

Pity for me.

"I appreciate everyone's concern for our relationship, but we don't need your input. We're doing just fine on our own," Jagger announces with finality. "Now, let's all go to the beach and have some fun today."

Everyone quickly agrees and heads toward the front door. Jagger smiles at me, no evidence of aggravation on his face. "Babe, can you grab the sunscreen from my bathroom? I'll get our towels and stuff together."

"Sure, Jagger."

After a few minutes of searching through the unorganized mess he calls a linen closet, I finally find the bottles of sunscreen. As soon as I step out of his bedroom, I hear hushed, angry voices in the kitchen. My curiosity gets the best of me, so I stop and secretly listen.

It's Cass and Jagger.

"Dane told me what you're doing to that poor girl," she accuses. "I can't believe you're my brother."

"What are you talking about?" he hisses back.

"Stringing her along until her dad signs you. Keeping her happy so she won't renege on the original agreement," she replies.

"How am I stringing her along? This agreement was her idea," he counters.

"But she left, Jagger. She walked away from you, ended this charade, and even then promised she'd keep her word," Cass says angrily. "The guys told you to pursue her, promise her the moon until you get what you're after. And you did just that, didn't you?"

Jagger doesn't reply.

"Then you announce to everyone that she's your girlfriend. You're making her believe this is real. When you and the band started this secret game, you changed the rules without telling her. You need to man up and tell her the truth," she says, disgusted.

"I can't," he glumly replies.

"Well then, I hope your fame and fortune are worth it when you can't bear to look in the mirror."

I jump back into his bedroom before she reaches the hall and realizes I've been listening. Never have I felt like such a fool before. Jagger is obviously a much better actor than I've given him credit for.

One more day. I'll just make it through one more day with him and then I'll never see him again. I'll end it with a text message. Realistically, there's no reason why I should stay and pretend. I'm evidently just a fucking glutton for punishment.

Time to put on my actress face.

"Jagger," I yell from his room just before I step into the hall. "Your bathroom closet is a mess. How do you stand it? I finally found the sunscreen you hid behind the five boxes of light bulbs."

Jagger is alone in the kitchen. I assume Cass walked out on him after her last comment. He's sitting at the table, staring at the floor, and his mind is a million miles away. Seeing his sister so upset with him must have really got to him. This is the side of him that he rarely shows.

"Ready to get this over with?" I ask casually but my phrasing is intentional.

When he raises his head, the sadness in his eyes almost makes me feel sorry for him. But I remind my stupid heart that it's not for me. It's for his sister and their relationship.

"We're running out of time," I add. Intentional again.

"Why are we running out of time?" he asks. His fake concern is Oscar worthy.

"Because you have a show to get ready for tonight." My tone of voice says DUH without having to actually add it.

"Right," he replies, dragging the one-syllable out to at least two or three. He may appear to agree, but he's more perceptive than he lets on. His tone says I'm not fooling him, but he won't push it right now.

JAGGER

The South Beach crowd is out in full force today. The beach is full of people and there's hardly any space near the water to claim as ours. Wes takes off ahead of us when he sees a group of girls in the perfect spot packing up their stuff. He starts up a conversation with them and invites them to our show tonight. When Mali and I reach them, they start to walk off when one of them stops when she sees me.

"Are you in the band, too?" She's obviously interested in me.

"Yeah, I'm the lead singer," I reply.

"In that case, I'll definitely be there tonight," she purrs. "I can't wait to spend the night with you…listening to you sing."

"New listeners are always welcome," I reply. I try to keep the banter light so I don't offend her, but I'm hyper-aware that Mali is right beside me.

The flirty girl nods, flashes me her seductive smile, and walks away.

"Holy shit, man. She's hot as fuck," Tanner says, as he nudges my arm.

"Man, watch how loud you say that shit," I angrily whisper, as I look over my shoulder at him.

"Why? No one's around," he points out.

I turn around to find Mali, but she's not there. Quickly searching the shoreline, I find her in ankle deep water, her face tilted up to soak in the sun. She's already removed her cover up and she's wearing the sexiest fucking bikini I've ever seen. It reveals just enough to be enticing but not give it all away. The bottoms don't completely cover the luscious cheeks of her perfectly tanned ass. Every guy that walks by her stops, turns around, and openly gawks at her body.

I'll end up killing some stupid fucker today.

Like this guy who finally works up the nerve to approach her. He touches her softly on the shoulder and she turns her head to look at him. The smile she gives him looks like the one she gives me when we're alone. I don't like this one fucking bit. He shouldn't get the same smile I get.

"Man, what's wrong with you?" Tanner asks. He follows my gaze and sees Mali.

"Holy shit. Her body is smoking hot," he loudly exclaims. "I've seen her in a bathing suit before, but not like that one. I think I need to be alone. With her."

"Stay the hell away from her, Tanner," my tone warns him.

He looks at me, hard, before his bottom jaw drops open. "You weren't lying before, were you? She really is your girlfriend."

"Don't start this shit with me right now," I dismiss him. Mali and the touchy-feely guy just walked further out into the water together. Whatever his plans for her are, they're about to be shot to hell by yours truly.

My stride is quick, my stance is aggressive, and my anger is seething on my way toward them. This obvious jealousy is so unlike me but I can't stop myself. I can hear their conversation just before I reach them. Her back is to me and he has no idea she's here with me.

"You honestly don't have a boyfriend?" he asks.

"No boyfriend," she replies.

"But you are seeing someone?" He sounds disappointed. Good.

She shakes her head side to side. "Just occasionally. It's not serious."

"I'd say it's time for you to dump him," the prick suggests. "If he doesn't want to take you completely off the market, he's an idiot."

"You may be right."

He doesn't know her well enough to recognize the sadness in her voice, but I do. I could punch him in the mouth, threaten to stuff and mount his balls like a trophy above my fireplace, and throw Mali over my shoulder to carry her off like a caveman. The problem is, his mouth spoke the truth about me. I don't have a fireplace because I live in Miami–it's hot as hell here. I'd still consider stuffing and mounting his balls like a trophy for touching her, though. And, most of all, Mali has to want to be with me on her own terms.

Maybe it's time I give her a reason to want to be.

She doesn't feel me approaching as I ease up behind her. The prick realizes I'm close to them, but not in enough time to warn Mali. I hook one arm behind her knees, sweep her feet out from under her, and support her back with my other arm. She squeals in surprise and flails in my arms for a second, so I hug her closer to me. Realization dawns and she looks up at me ruefully as she hooks her arm around my neck.

"Jagger, you scared the hell out of me," she laughingly admonishes. "Don't you know better than to sneak up on someone in the ocean?"

"Guess I missed that memo," I smile. "And I missed you. You disappeared on me."

"You were busy talking with your new fan," she replies. "I didn't want to intrude."

One thing I've always hated and tried to avoid is a clingy, needy girl. The type that gets jealous when I talk to another female. One time, my date was instantly threatened because a ninety-year-old grandma asked me for the time. Ridiculous behavior. So why does it bother me that there's no jealousy or cattiness in Mali's voice? She walked off and left me alone with the flirty girl without a backward glance.

"She was the one who intruded. I didn't want to be rude to a potential new fan. But, that doesn't mean I didn't want you there."

"Hey, man," the prick interrupts. "The lady and I were having a conversation."

"Oh, dude, I'm sorry," I reply, being completely facetious. "Please continue."

Mali is still in my arms with her arm around my neck and we're both waiting for the prick to dazzle us with his conversational skills. So far, I have to say I'm less than impressed. Tilting my head slightly to the side, I raise my brows in an attempt to cue him.

"Where were we?" The prick speaks. Finally.

"I believe you were at the part where you called me an idiot," I answer.

"How could I call you an idiot when I didn't even know you?"

"You said she should dump me because I'm an idiot for not taking her off the market," I remind him. "So, you can pick up there and finish giving us the rest of your invaluable advice."

"Whatever, man," he replies. Frustrated, he gives up and leaves us alone in the ocean.

When Mali looks up at me, I know without a doubt that something is wrong. What she said to that prick stung, but I can't blame her for it. She can't hide the pain in her eyes. I bend my knees, lower my body into the water, and set her on my legs. Now we're face to face and away from everyone else.

"What's wrong, Mali? Talk to me," I gently urge her.

"Nothing," she lies.

She glides through the water effortlessly as I turn her to face me. Her legs wrap around my waist and I cover her mouth with mine. She hesitates at first, but I feel her entire body relax as she stops fighting and engages in our kiss. I thread my arms under hers and cross

148

them on her back, pulling her tightly to me. Skin on skin, there's barely enough room for a droplet of water to pass between us.

When I break the kiss, I hold her face with both of my hands. "Mali, please talk to me. I know something's bothering you."

"I don't like the lies," she replies cryptically.

She's done this a few other times, phrasing her response so that can be interpreted in multiple ways.

"What lies, specifically?"

She takes a minute to answer, but I wait patiently.

"Yours."

"Mine? What have I lied to you about?"

"Let's not do this now," she avoids answering me. "We should just enjoy the time we have."

"We're not finished with this conversation," I state. "If I've done something, you can at least give me a chance to explain or make up for it."

"You can make up for it," she tries to distract me.

Her hand moves between my legs and strokes me through my shorts. It's not a terrible plan, as far as distractions go. I may give her fifteen minutes or so to stop doing it, just for good measure. "I thought you needed my help to become braver. Here you are, trying to have your way with me out in public," I tease.

"What can I say? You naturally bring out the bad girl in me."

What worries me is, the way she said it doesn't sound like her bad girl will be good for me.

CHAPTER THIRTEEN

MALI

We went to the club last night and, like a good little Jagger York groupie, I watched him perform, play up to the female fans that lined the front row of the stage, and fight off about a hundred girls after the show. The funny thing is, after the show he had every chance to leave my side, but he didn't. Girls came out of the woodwork with excuses why they needed his help, something that he was the only man in the universe equipped to handle, but he refused every one of them.

His hand held onto mine, his arm was wrapped around me, or his lips were on mine the entire time. There was even one song he sang to me as we sat in the booth, drinking beer and munching on appetizers. His parents left a note that it was their date night and they wouldn't be back. Cass left with Dane after the show was over and said we shouldn't expect her either. That meant Jagger's place would be completely empty for the night.

The warm water of his pool felt divine against my bare skin. Even after spending all week in the water, I never tire of it. My parents have joked that I was a mermaid in a past life because I live in the water and visit dry land. Last night, skinny-dipping with Jagger left me with a new appreciation for the water, underwater acrobatics, and creative ways to use pool noodles.

Knowing this day has been inevitable from the start doesn't make it one ounce easier. Over the past few weeks, I've gotten to know every side of Jagger. His sweet, thoughtful side, the playful, boyish side, and the deceitful, fake side. My favorite, though, is the vulnerable, genuine aspect that he hides beneath his obnoxious stage persona. He doesn't let it show often, but I've seen it and that's the part of him that I'm keeping with me.

It's five a.m. on Sunday morning and Jagger is still fast asleep. He was so worn out after his show, followed by our late night swim, and then a repeat in his bedroom, that he didn't feel me leave the bed. Even if he didn't know my intent, I held nothing back as I made love to him last night. With every touch, every movement, and every utterance, I gave him my heart. Did he steal my heart, or did I willingly hand it over? Either way, it's his now.

He didn't hear me gathering my things. He didn't realize I was getting dressed. And he won't know I'm gone for several hours yet. I can't help but stare at him one last time before I walk out. I haven't slept at all tonight and I'll pay for it while I'm at practice all day. All I could do was stare at his gorgeous face as he slept and wonder if he has any clue how completely in love with him I am.

In my mind, I tell him all the things I'd never say to his face. *You were my hero in the club that night. You took care of me when you didn't have to. You've helped me step out of my sheltered world, but you don't fully realize it. Even though this started as a fake relationship, it's ending as something very real to me. I'll never forget you, Jagger York.*

One thing I never told him was why I had to go out of town and miss practice those few days. I took his band's CD to my dad personally and asked him to listen to it. We spent time together, just talking about my future and what happens if I don't make the cut to go to the Olympic preliminaries. It's a very real possibility since there are only six spots open for women and six for men per country, and there over twenty thousand competitive divers in the U.S. who would love to have a spot. Past performance is a major factor in being selected for the team, and so is current skill level compared to the other competitors.

I've replayed the discussion with my father over and over in my mind…

"Hi, Daddy." I smiled as I entered his enormous office, unannounced and unexpected.

Surprise registered on his face, quickly followed by joy to see me. "Hey, Precious," he smiled brightly as he used his pet name for me. "What in the world are you doing here?"

"I have something I want you to listen to. I know you well enough to know that I have to be here in person to make you listen to it," I laughed.

"My secret is out. It's the only way I get to see you," he joked. "Give your old daddy a hug."

I wrapped my arms around his neck and squeezed him tightly. "I've missed you," I said as I kissed his cheek.

"I've missed you, too, baby girl," he replied. When we stepped back, he continued. "This must be pretty important to you since you're missing dive practice right now." He quirked one eyebrow up and quickly assessed me. "And you have a long flight back to Miami…from LAX."

"It is," I replied. "I need your full attention to it."

"You got it," he promised. "Let's hear it."

I walked over to his stereo and put the CD in and then took a seat in front of his desk. He turned the volume up using his remote, leaned his head back in his huge, leather chair, and closed his eyes. Jagger's voice filled the room as he crooned his own eclectic blend of different music genres. After a few songs had played, Daddy opened his eyes and paused the music.

"They're pretty good," he nodded. "How did you come into possession of this particular band's music?"

"That's classified. I could tell you but then I'd have to kill you. Courts frown on children killing their parent," I smiled.

He laughed, knowing I was only teasing him, and shook his head. "Yes, they do. And fathers frown on their daughters flying from coast to coast for a fifteen minute meeting."

"It could be longer," I offered. "You could listen to the whole thing."

"I don't need to hear any more. Leave me his contact information and I'll be in touch soon. Don't expect it in the next three to four weeks, though. I have a contract negotiation and a new release being mixed, so I can't start anything new just yet."

"Promise me, Daddy," I said solemnly, knowing how he frequently changed his mind or forgot if too much time passed. "I need to hear the words."

He sighed heavily but indulged me. "I promise, Mali. In three or four weeks–five at the most–I will give him a call."

"Thank you, Daddy. You're the best."

"I try for my little girl. How long are you staying?"

"A couple of days. I've already cleared it with my coach, but I had to agree to practice the next two weekends to make up for it," I replied half-heartedly.

"Be careful, Mali," he replied softly.

"I'll be fine." I nodded, but we both knew he wasn't referring to my training schedule.

The soft clicking of the door locking behind me sealed my decision. There's no way to get back inside now even if I changed my mind. I started my car, backed out of his driveway without turning my headlights on, and drove away. My plan was to drive away without looking back, as a symbolic gesture to myself. But I couldn't do it. I had to know if he'd noticed my absence yet. Like a scene from a romance movie, part of me hoped he was running barefoot down the street behind my car, calling my name, begging me to come back.

His dark house showed no signs of movement. No indication that my absence had been detected. I saw nothing to suggest that I was the least bit missed. Dragging my eyes from my rearview mirror, I focused on the road ahead of me, and where it would take me. I'd always planned my future out, took the steps I needed to achieve my goals, and even though I have Olympic aspirations, I approach it realistically. Up until this idea, I've always taken the mature route. I suppose I'm allowed one enormous fuck up in my life.

When I reach the condo, I quickly shower, pack a bag with enough to last a few days, and head straight to the training facility. After a quick Google search, I dial the number and the call is answered on the second ring.

"Grand Beach Hotel. How can I help you?" the friendly girl answers.

"I'd like to make a reservation, please," I reply.

"I'll be glad to help you with that. When are you arriving?"

"Today. I'd like an oceanfront corner room, if possible," I reply.

"For how many nights?"

"Three," I reply after deliberating for a couple of seconds.

After taking my name and credit card information, she confirmed my stay and promised my room would be ready as requested. On autopilot, I reached the pool, changed into my bathing suit for diving, and started my practice early. The busier I stay, the easier it is to keep the sad thoughts away. I climb the stairs to the ten-meter platform first to start practicing the various high dives. When I surface after the first dive, slow clapping startles me.

"You're here early," Coach Platt says. "Couldn't sleep?"

As I haul myself out of the water, I nod. "Something like that."

"That was excellent form, Mali. You're more focused this morning than I've seen you lately," he comments.

"I'm working on that."

"Keep that up and you have a shot." He smiles and walks on toward his office.

I make the steady climb up the flights of stairs to the high platform and do it all over again. And again. And again.

JAGGER

"You've got to be fucking kidding me," I yell as I stomp through the house. Checking the back deck for the fourth time doesn't produce any new results. "I can't believe she's gone."

I've called her phone repeatedly but she hasn't answered. Being the attentive, considerate boyfriend that I am, I don't even know which pool she practices at because I never bothered to ask. She took all of her things with her and didn't say goodbye. She's been gone since long before her normal practice time because she wasn't here when I woke up early. I reached for her... to hold her while we slept... because I've turned into a pussy-whipped moron.

That was two hours ago and I still can't reach her. I eventually called the guard's station at her condo, told him I couldn't reach her and I was concerned she'd been in a wreck or something. He finally told me she'd already been there and left again. I've been pacing back and forth for probably the past hour when my parents show up.

"Jagger, what's wrong?" Mom asks when she's sees the wild look in my eyes.

"Something's wrong with Mali. I know it, I feel it, but she won't talk to me." I've admitted defeat. I'm talking to my mom about my girlfriend.

"Maybe she wants more from you than your current arrangement," Dad says.

"What do you mean?" I ask.

"Maybe she wants you to actually tell her that you want her to be your real girlfriend and not just your pretend one," he elaborates.

"How do you know about that?" I'm going to kill Cass.

"I heard you tell Cass about your arrangement," he admits. "But you were too focused on yourself to see Mali honestly cares about you."

"That wasn't supposed to happen. It was her idea," I defend myself. "That doesn't mean that I don't care about her, too."

"If you never told her, how was she supposed to know?" he asks. Rhetorically, I'm sure, since he already knows the answer.

My chin drops to my chest as I hang my head in shame. Of course he's right. Cass was right, too. "She won't take my call. I'm sure she's at diving practice right now, but I don't think she'll answer it later, either."

"Then I guess you better find another way to get through to her." Dad gives me a pat on the shoulder as he and Mom walk back to their bedroom.

"Oh, by the way, we found a house. We'll be out of your way in a couple of weeks," he says.

"No need to rush," I reply with all sincerity.

Two days later, she still hasn't answered my calls. She hasn't even returned to her condo. The only way I know she's okay is because Jennifer feels sorry for me in my current deranged state. Even Joey, the club owner, has noticed a difference in my demeanor on stage. My heart just isn't in it right now. Cass and Dane have something going on. While they try to make me feel better, they're obviously becoming more than just a passing fling. That doesn't help.

Mom and Dad just left for their date night, Cass and Dane are out doing whatever they do, and I'm sitting here all alone. When my phone rings with an unknown number, my heart skips a beat at the possibility it's Mali calling me.

"Hello?" I answer expectantly.

"Is this Jagger York?" an older man's voice asks.

"Yeah. Who's this?"

"This is Milo Greyson. I'd like to meet with you about your music. I happen to be in Miami right now. Can you meet me at Casa Tua at seven tonight?" he asks.

"That's great news, Mr. Greyson. I'll be glad to meet with you," I reply.

"When you get here, just tell the hostess you're here with me. She'll bring you upstairs to the members-only area. I'll see you soon."

We hang up and I rush to dress appropriately for the most expensive restaurant in Miami. It stings that Mali kept her word even though she won't speak to me now. Either she's trying to help get me signed to get rid of me, or she's an even better person than I gave her credit for. Either way, I'm fucked.

When I reach the restaurant, the hostess immediately recognizes Milo's name and escorts me to the ultra-exclusive area upstairs. Milo stands to shake my hand as we officially introduce ourselves.

"Milo Greyson. Nice to meet you," he says politely, although a little cool.

"Jagger York," I reply. "It's nice to meet you, too."

"Have a seat," he gestures.

"I have to say, I was surprised to hear from you," I start the conversation. "How did you come across our music?"

"My daughter personally brought your CD to me a few weeks ago," he replies.

I can literally feel the color drain from my face. That must have been over the days when she missed practice. "I didn't know she personally delivered it."

He nods, and his expression says he figured as much. "The thing is, Jagger, I do like your style. Your music is unique, as Mali said. There are some technical issues I think we can work out, but overall I'm interested in producing your music. I'll have to hear the individual musicians myself before making a commitment."

"We'll be glad to play for you while you're in town. We can either do it in the club where we have a standing gig or in a professional studio," I offer.

"One thing I know about my daughter is she wouldn't have brought it to me herself if she didn't care about you," Milo says.

Now we're getting to the real point of this meeting.

"The truth is, Jagger, I've been around guys like you for more than thirty years. Every one of you guys think you're different, that you broke the mold, when the truth is you're all the same. Mali's beautiful, smart, talented, and she's going places. But with the Greyson last name, she's also a high-profile target for someone who wants to use her to get to me. You may not have exploited her last name, but I think you have taken advantage of it.

"Here's what I'm willing to do. If you walk away and leave her alone for good, I'll listen to your band. Your singing has already sold me. If you agree to my terms, you're in. I'm not convinced one of your musicians is ready to be in the limelight, though. We may have to replace him with someone more experienced."

My head is spinning. He's willing to sign me if I stay away from his daughter forever, but I also have to give up one of my band members. This is too much to comprehend all at once.

"What do you say, son?" he asks.

He hasn't looked away from me since I arrived. He's watched my every movement, assessed my every response, and sized me up in a matter of minutes. I think he already knows what my answer is.

"Had you asked me to stay away from a specific girl a few weeks ago in exchange for a deal with you, I would've jumped at the offer without a second thought," I start. "But, even then, I wouldn't have just turned my back on one of my best friends.

"Today, after spending time with Mali and really getting to know her, I'd never promise you or anyone else that I wouldn't contact her again. I'd love for you to come listen to us as musicians, tell us where improvements can be made, but I won't agree to kick one of my friends out of the band. If that type of decision were to ever be made, the whole band, not just me, would make it.

"But since Mali is part of your package deal, I assume the whole deal is off the table and there's nothing else we need to talk about."

I push my chair back from the table and stand. "Before I leave, you should know that I plan to do everything in my power to win her back. They say you don't know what you've got until it's gone. I say sometimes what you had was nothing you were looking for, but everything you need, only you don't realize it until it's gone. That's what Mali is to me."

Without another word, I turn and walk away from him and head for the stairs.

"Hold up, son," he calls.

I keep walking. I'm not in the mood for games.

"I said hold up, Jagger," he says more forcefully.

Anger boils inside me as I turn and look at him. "What?"

"You'll find her here." He hands me a card with a handwritten address on it. "She'll be at dive practice all day tomorrow at PureEnergy Aquatics, but she's staying at this hotel right now."

He gives me her room number and wishes me luck. "Oh, and bring the boys to Greyson Recording Studios tomorrow afternoon at two. We'll talk about your contract terms. I would invite you to stay and have dinner with me, but I have a feeling you have somewhere else you'd rather be right now."

"Yes, I definitely do. Thank you, sir."

CHAPTER FOURTEEN

MALI

All I really want to do is sleep, but I only see Jagger when I lie down, so I haven't really slept the past two nights. Practice started late today because the crew cleaned the pool first thing this morning. My coach doesn't let stuff like that cut practice short, so every member of the dive team is here late tonight. I've been at this for so many hours today I can barely feel my muscles now. Yet, I'm still climbing the three stories to the high platform to jump off of it and perform aerial acrobatics on my way down to the fifteen feet of water below.

"Mali," Coach Platt calls to me. "Are you okay?"

"I'm fine," I lie. "Why do you ask?"

"I think you've had enough for today. Why don't you come back down the stairs instead?" he replies.

"I'm fine, Coach," I insist.

He crosses his arms over his chest and gives me a dubious look. When he doesn't persist, I take that as my cue to continue.

Honestly, I would have anyway because if it appears I can't handle the grueling schedule, he'll cut me from the team. As I approach the edge of the platform, I picture the twists, turns, and positions my body has to be in to execute it flawlessly. Then I jump, and my muscles remember the moves with precision.

As I exit the pool, I throw my *I told you so look* over my shoulder at Coach Platt. He replies with his usual sarcasm, "That'll do."

Laughing, I walk to the hot tub and sink into the hot water. It helps to keep my muscles loose and limber to perform the dives after being in the cooler pool water. Stretching my arms, shoulders, and back, I loosen up my stiff muscles to prepare for the next dive. Every step is harder to take than the last, but I finally reach the platform. I walk to the edge, get into a handstand position, and mentally prepare for my acrobatics.

The flips, twists, and turns come so naturally that I don't think much about them anymore. But as I bring my arms straight above my head, I instinctively know something is off. Subconsciously I knew pushing myself wasn't such a good idea. I'm not firing on all cylinders and diving is too dangerous to not be at my absolute best. As I enter the water at close to forty miles per hour, one arm is tipped too far backward and it feels like it just slammed into a concrete wall when I hit the water.

The loud pop echoes underwater simultaneous with the intensely sharp pain of my shoulder forcefully being shoved backward in an unnatural position. From the excruciating pain, my immediate guess is it's now dislocated since I've seen it happen to other divers before. My feet touch the bottom of the deep pool but it feels like I'm in suspended animation. My lungs burn as they furiously urge me to exhale the breath I'm holding and inhale fresh oxygen. But I don't. I should be kicking my feet to propel my body toward the surface. Instead, I'm watching my dreams of winning an Olympic medal dissolve in the water, within sight but just out of my reach. Those dreams have been in the forefront of my mind for so many years, but now I helplessly watch them float away into oblivion.

Strong arms wrap around my waist and pull me toward the surface of the water. My lungs sting as we rise but my eyes are fixed on the bottom of the pool, where I've left all my years of practice and sacrifice. When we break the surface, my automatic functions take over where my conscious mind has failed me and compel me to resume inhaling and exhaling normally. The pain in my shoulder hits me full force and I grit my teeth to keep from screaming loudly.

More arms come from different directions to pull me out of the pool and set me on the concrete that surrounds it. Holding my arm close to my body, I lower my chin to my chest and let the tears fall. Tears from physical pain, yes, but the mental pain of this truth hurts just as much.

"Mali," a commanding voice yells at me. "Answer me!"

When I raise my eyes, I question if I'm hallucinating as I gaze into the chocolate brown eyes of Jagger. He's fully clothed, soaking wet, and still stands on the pool ladder as he leans over toward me.

In my current state, none of this makes sense to me. *Why is Jagger in the pool?*

"Baby, talk to me," he says concerned. "What happened? Are you okay?"

"She had her arm too far back when she hit the water," Coach Platt explains. "That type of impact can dislocate the shoulder."

"It doesn't look out of place," Jagger replies.

"It may not have completely dislocated. It could've popped out and then slid back in place," Coach Platt replies. "Let's get her dried off and take her to have it looked at."

Jagger steps out of the pool, stoops down behind me, and wraps his arms around my waist. "I'll help you up, baby," he says lovingly. The timbre of his voice assures me. Even soaking wet, his embrace warms me. His presence calms my frazzled nerves.

"You're really here?" I ask with a trembling whisper.

"I'm here," he whispers back, nuzzling my neck. "I'm not leaving you."

He pulls me to stand and my legs feel like jelly, but I gingerly walk toward the door anyway. Putting one foot in front of the other without jarring the rest of my body is much harder than I ever imagined. The impact each time my foot strikes the ground shoots through my torso and straight to my injured shoulder.

The assistants shove towels at us as we walk by and Jagger carefully wraps one around my shoulders. He uses his to dry his hair off, haphazardly rubbing it across his head and instantly styling his hair perfectly. When we reach his truck, he helps me get settled in before he grabs a bag from the backseat. Standing in the parking lot with the driver side door open, he sheds his wet clothes, throws

171

them in the back, and pulls on a dry T-shirt and shorts.

"I'll drive as carefully as I can, but I can't avoid every bump in the road. I'm apologizing ahead of time because it's going to kill me every time I cause you more pain," he says sincerely.

"I'll be okay, Jagger," I lie. We both know this ride will hurt like hell.

JAGGER

Mali has been home from the hospital for a week now. That night still replays in my nightmares and wakes me up at night...

After I met with her father at the restaurant, I went straight to the hotel to see her and make her talk to me. After checking twice for her car, I decided to drive over to PureEnergy Aquatics to see if she was still practicing by some off chance. It was already much later than she normally practiced, but I quickly found her car in the parking lot. As I neared the door, I saw the key card scanner that prevented unauthorized people from getting inside. I caught a lucky break when a couple of girls walked out, saw me jogging toward the door, and politely held the door for me to enter. They walked away giggling after I gave them my best smile and thanked them.

Once inside, it was easy to find the Olympic size pool with the multiple tiered platforms. I've watched the competitions on TV before, where the camera zooms in on the diver before following them down to the water below. Of course, the camera pans out and shows the whole scene occasionally, but my focus has always been on the person diving. Now that I'm standing in this enormous facility, I'm in complete shock and awe at how high the dive platform is. My girl has been repeatedly jumping off this thing?

That's when I saw her climbing the stairs toward the top platform. After moving as close as I could get without calling attention to myself, I took a seat and watched her every move. She looked so tired–I could see that even from as far away as I sat. But her determination and grit were still evident. As she approached the edge, I held my breath and waited for her to willingly jump off. Her coach tried to get her to take a break, so he obviously didn't think she should go through with this one. But she insisted, and he relented. My hands curled into tight fists as I anxiously waited.

Then she jumped and it was absolutely beautiful. Stunning. Amazing. Perfect ten. Or whatever score they give for diving, I don't even know. I thought she'd be done after that one, especially after her coach's suggestion, but she walked back to the stairs again after a couple of minutes. I nearly jumped up and yelled, *"What the fuck are you doing?"* when she walked to the very edge of the platform and did a perfect handstand. As she teetered on the edge of a thirty-foot high concrete platform, I sat there and helplessly watched her.

She propelled herself off the edge, turned, flipped, and maneuvered her body with precision. My bottom jaw hung open and my eyes bulged from their sockets. It was the most amazing sight I'd ever witnessed in person. Pride swelled in my chest for her as I said aloud, "There's no way she won't make the Olympic team. Look at her."

Immediately before she touched the water, her coach was urgently rushing toward the side of the pool. I had no idea what was wrong, but he obviously sensed something very bad was about to happen. He was the coach, he knew best, so I jumped up from my seat and rushed to get closer.

174

Once her fingers touched the water, it was like she was suddenly swallowed by the depths and my heart sank. Her coach yelled, "Mali! Mali!" just as I reached his side. I think my heart stopped when I looked in the deep pool and saw her at the bottom, not moving. The coach began to kick his shoes off, but I couldn't wait that long. Fully clothed, I plunged into the water and pulled her to the surface.

The drive to the hospital was rough on Mali, as I knew it would be. Every little bump and pothole in the road magnified her pain twenty times over.

"I'm sorry, baby," I said every time she winced in pain.

"It's not your fault, Jagger," she replied every time.

When the nurse called her name to take her back to an examination room, I got up to go with her. I said I wasn't leaving her and I meant it. The nurse gave me a doubtful look as she confirmed with Mali. "Is he family?"

"Yes, I am," I replied.

"Yes," Mali confirmed.

She still didn't look convinced but she didn't push it. When she left, I helped Mali change into a dry hospital gown, lay on the bed, and she carefully moved until she had positioned herself in a way that didn't hurt more.

"Do you want me to call your dad?" I asked.

Disbelief flashed across her features before complete sadness overtook her eyes. "You're worried about my dad *now*? What can he do from California?" she asked, anger simmering just under her pain.

"What? No, that's not what I meant. He's here in Miami. I just met with him today," I explained. "You didn't know?"

Surprise and confusion replaced the sadness. "No, I haven't talked to him. But then, I haven't checked my phone since I got to practice earlier this morning."

"So, do you want me to call him? Tell him you're here?"

"No. It's not life or death, so I'd rather wait until we know more," she decided.

"Mali-," I began, just as the door opened and someone interrupted me.

"Ms. Greyson, it's time for your x-ray," the lady announced. When she looked at me, she continued. "I'm Barbara and I'm an x-ray tech. I'm taking her to radiology and I'll bring her back to this room. Just wait here for her."

I nodded and stood as Barbara wheeled Mali's gurney out of the room and down the hall. While she was in radiology, I paced back in forth in the emergency room. My wet shoes squished with every step. The noise drew curious looks from others and reminded me of how lifeless she looked on the bottom of that pool. Something my dad said to me instantly came to mind and everything made sense.

"Jagger?" her weak voice called from behind me.

When I turned, my beautiful girl was being wheeled back into her room. "I'm here, Mali. I'm not going anywhere," I reassured her again. I walked in behind her and watched as the nurse gave her something for her pain. I sat down beside her bed, stuck my arm through the bars on the side rail, and held her good hand.

"Thank you," she whispered as she squeezed my hand.

"For what?"

"Staying," she said. As she closed her eyes and allowed the pain medicine to take over, a single tear ran down her temple and disappeared into her hairline.

"You don't seem to get it," I whisper as she drifts to sleep. "I'm never leaving you."

It's been one week since that night and I'm driving her to her follow up doctor's appointment. She's still protesting.

"Jagger, seriously, I can drive myself."

"I know you can. But so can I."

"My shoulder wasn't even out of place. Just an extremely painful and scary strain. It's so much better now that I don't even need the sling anymore," she says as she moves her arm around. "Going to physical therapy has really helped me strengthen it."

"You were too tired, Mali. Your body was beyond fatigued and you needed this week to rest. So lean back, relax, and rest on the way to the doctor's office," I demand.

"Fine," she huffs. "You missed your appointment with my dad, you know."

"It's okay. He really wanted to hear the guys play anyway. He said he was sold on my voice either way," I reply. "Besides, someone had to move your stuff out of that hotel room and back to your condo."

She nods but doesn't say anything else. The reminder of why she was in that hotel room still hangs in the air between us. The first few days after her injury, she was still on pain medicine. I need her to be completely lucid when I tell her what I have to say. The past couple of days when I tried to broach the subject, she completely shut me down. So I'm waiting for the opportune moment.

"We're here," I announce. "Let me get your door."

"I can do it," she protests. Again. I rush around to help her anyway. At least my attempts earn a smile from her.

After getting an all clear from her doctor, she calls her coach and gives him the good news. He orders her to take it easy through the weekend and then show up to resume practice next Monday. She tries to argue with him because the final meet to determine who goes to the Olympic preliminaries is in less than two weeks.

"What did he say?" I ask when she hangs up.

"He said for me to trust him. That I'll do better when I'm rested and focused," she huffs.

"He has a point, you know."

"The doctor completely released me," she says. "So you're free move back to your house now. There's no reason for you to stay and take care of me anymore. You've taken off work long enough and missed enough important appointments in your own life."

I wasn't expecting that as a reply in the least. All I can do is nod, like I agree with her. Which I don't. "Yeah, he did release you."

The elevator ride up to her condo is quiet and strained. When we step inside, she starts picking up my belongings from the various rooms and putting them all in one spot. She's making it easy for me to just throw my shit in my suitcase and walk away.

"Mali, I need to talk to you," I state.

"Jagger," she sighs. "I don't want to do this."

"Too fucking bad, because I do," I reply angrily. "I do want to do this. I want this with you."

"No, you don't," she angrily replies. "I overheard you and Cass in your kitchen, Jagger. I know that you agreed to do or say whatever it takes to keep me until you and your band get signed. I appreciate everything you've done since I injured my shoulder, but we're through pretending."

"I'm not pretending. You want to hear something funny? After I told you not to get attached to me, I'm the one who's now permanently attached to you. My dad gave me some advice after he met you. He said if I couldn't stand the thought of you being with another man, then you meant more to me than I acknowledged.

"But it's more than that, Mali. Just the thought of never being able to hold you again is enough to bring me to my knees. I can't picture my life without you in it–not today, next week, or in the future. It's not just that I've missed you, it's that part of me is missing without you. The things that were so important to me before are not so important now if I have to lose you to gain them."

She's like a beautiful statue, standing motionless. Her eyes remain glued to me as I pace back and forth during my confession. Strolling straight to her, my expression hungry and determined, I cup her face in my hands and hold her attention.

"Are you listening to me, Mali?" I ask. "I'm going to tell you something very important and I need you to hear every word."

She nods slightly but remains silent. Her eyes search mine and silently plead with me for reassurance that she can trust me.

"I love you, Mali. I am so head over heels, wrapped around your little finger, turn in my fucking man-card, put my balls in your pink purse, in love with you. Don't give up on us," I all but beg her.

"You weren't trying to trick me when you said I was your girlfriend?" she asks, her voice thick with emotion.

"No, baby, I wasn't tricking you at all. Don't let what you heard Cass say come between us. I've been fighting this feeling almost since the first night I met you. The more I got to know you, the more I knew it'd be impossible to walk away from you. I'm sorry for hurting you, though, and I promise to spend forever making it up to you," I vow.

"I love you, Jagger," she says, her eyes brimming with tears. "I really want to believe you, but I don't want to be hurt again."

"Never, Mali. I'll never hurt you again. I'll do whatever it takes to prove that to you. Let me show you."

EPILOGUE

MALI

AUGUST

The week off from practice was beneficial in more ways than one. My mind and body really did need the rest. When I went back to diving, I performed better than ever. The qualifying tournament was a huge success and I made the cut for the Olympic preliminary competition. Now, I have a year to prepare to compete against the best of the best from every country to earn a spot on the final Olympic team.

"Jagger," I call from the deck, "you're going to burn the steaks."

"Back away from my grill, woman," he teases as he steps out the sliding glass door. "You have my balls in your pink purse, but I maintain control of the grill. That was the agreement."

"You and your agreements," I roll my eyes.

"It was *your* idea," he counters. "It's the end of summer, you know. Should we make a new agreement now?"

"You two act like you're already married," Dane interjects. "You should just go make it official because we all know you're going to anyway."

"Stop rushing us," Jagger points the grilling fork at Dane. "We'll get married when Mali says we're good and ready."

Dane and Cass bust out in laughter at Jagger's humor. It's actually one of the first things I fell in love with about him. That and how he saved me that night. How he makes me feel impetuous and brave. How he makes love to me. How he's turned me into a raging nymphomaniac. The list goes on and on.

"I know that look, Mali," he lowers his voice and leans in whisper in my ear. "I'll let the damn steaks burn all day if you look at me like that again."

"Maybe Dane and Cass aren't that hungry anyway," I suggest.

Jagger growls and extends his arm to throw the grilling fork across the deck when Cass stops him.

"Yes, Dane and Cass are that hungry. Don't overcook my steak, Jagger," she warns.

Jagger points at me. "You're making this up to me later when *they* finally leave," he emphasizes 'they' loudly so that 'they' hear him.

"My pleasure," I reply. "Actually, it'll be your pleasure, too. But you know what I mean."

"I do believe I've been a bad influence on you, Miss Greyson," Jagger quips.

"I agree. But I wouldn't change it for anything in the world," I smile just before his mouth covers mine.

"Jagger," Cass yells, "my steak!"

JAGGER

ONE YEAR LATER

"Holy shit," I exclaim. "I'm more nervous than she is. How can she be so calm at a time like this? Doesn't she know what this means?"

"Jagger, if you don't sit down and shut up, I'll be forced to duct tape you to that chair," Milo threatens me. "No court would convict me."

Mali takes her place on the platform again. She jumps off of a perfectly sound structure and hurtles her body toward the water below. Her body is bent in an unnatural shape with her chest touching her thighs. Her form is so perfect that not even a speck of light could fit in between. She performs one somersault after another, before straightening and entering the water with barely a splash. Her cheering section at the Olympic preliminaries goes crazy with screams, whistles, noisemakers, and flashing signs with her name written with bold permanent markers.

"She still doesn't know about your decision?" Milo asks.

"No, I didn't want to tell her before this tournament. It wouldn't be fair to put that kind pressure on her," I reply to Milo, but keep my eyes on the love of my life that's exiting the pool right now.

"You're a good man, Jagger," he pats me on the shoulder.

"Only because she made me want to be a better man."

My parents, Cass, Dane, Milo, and Mandy, Mali's mother, are here with us to support Mali's dreams of Olympic gold. Her scores from each of the judges flash up on the board and I immediately search Mali's face for her reaction. I'm still learning how everything is scored. I don't even know how the judges see her form with her body moving at about forty miles per hour, all while twirling, twisting, and spinning.

At the end of the competition, Mali walks straight into my waiting arms, buries her face in my chest, and I try to console her. "I'm so sorry, baby. I thought you were the best one here," I tell her sincerely. "I'm proud of you. No matter what."

"You can be proud of yourself, Mali. Not many people ever even get this far. This is a great accomplishment," Milo says as he looks around the enormous facility. "I love you, baby girl."

"Mali, you kicked ass out there. Do you want me to kick those judges' asses? Because I'll do it," Dane offers.

Mali gets a chuckle from this and turns to reply to everyone. "Thank you for coming, everyone. I really appreciate it. I can honestly say that I did my best here today and held nothing back. It really sucks to not have made the team, but I can only say it just wasn't meant to be."

At the end of the night, after we've all enjoyed dinner together and relived the highlights of the day, we go our separate ways to our hotel rooms. As we say our goodnights, Milo raises his eyebrows at me and inclines his head toward Mali in his silent command to approach her about it now.

I nod in agreement. It's now or never.

Inside our room, I wrap my arms around her from behind and hold her close to me. "I love you, Mali."

"I love you, too, Jagger," she replies sweetly.

"We need to talk, baby."

"What kind of talk? Dirty talk? Because I didn't really have a conversation in mind," she purrs.

"You know I love it when you take charge like that," I growl. "You're making this very hard."

"That's the point," she quips.

I've created a monster. A very beautiful, sexy, tempting, seducing monster.

"Mmmm, you have to stop that for the next five minutes. You're killing me," I warn her as my hands roam over her body. I'm only adding to my own frustration but she just feels too damn good.

"Okay, let's hear it," she says as she turns to face me. "You've been hiding something from me for a while now. What's on your mind?"

"How do you know?" I eye her suspiciously.

"Because I know you, Jagger. Spill it."

"All right," I sigh. "You know we've been recording our first full-length album over the past year. And our tour is slated to start this fall." She nods. "Well, if you'd made the team today, I arranged with your father to put the tour on hold so I could stay here and support you."

"You what?" she gasps. "Jagger, why would you do that?"

I smile. She doesn't know? "Because I love you more than anything, Mali. I meant it when I said part of me is missing when I'm not with you."

Beautiful tears slide down her face. Tears of love. Tears of happiness. She rushes to me and repeatedly kisses my face. My arms wrap around her and hold her close to me. "I love you so much, Jagger. You're all that I need and want. I don't know what I'd do without you. I'd be so lost," she says as she lovingly strokes my face. "What happens now that I didn't make the team?" she asks.

"How would you like to go on tour with me and the band? For just one fall?"

The End

ABOUT THE AUTHOR

A.D. Justice is happily married to her husband of twenty-five years. They have two sons together and enjoy a wide variety of outdoor activities. A.D. has a full-time job by day, with a BS degree in Organizational Management and an MBA in Health Care Administration. Writing gives her the outlet she needs to live in the fantasy world that is a constant in her mind.

Thank you for reading and supporting A.D.'s books! Please take a moment to leave a review of this work.

You can find her online at:
FB:
https://www.facebook.com/adjusticeauthor
Twitter: https://twitter.com/ADJustice1
Web: www.adjusticebooks.com
Email: adjustice@outlook.com

www.ingramcontent.com/pod-product-compliance
Lightning Source LLC
Chambersburg PA
CBHW032134170626
46808CB00006B/2233